GAIL MCPHERSON

Lifting the Fog

Once Upon an Emotion - Book 3

Foreword

Welcome dear reader! Before we step into Farrah's tale, allow me to introduce those who will guide her on this profound journey.

Firstly, her steadfast friends - Willa, whose loyalty never falters even when Farrah retreats fully into despair and Edgar, whose quiet kindness becomes a lantern through her darkest nights. The wise mentor - Ignitus, an ancient phoenix, teaches Farrah that no darkness is endless.

And you, dear reader, shall walk alongside Farrah too in spirit. For though her road is fantastical, her struggle is universal. All who have faced adversity and longing will recognize her quest to rekindle lost light.

These are the guides who shall accompany our fairy's profound journey. Their presence serves to remind us that no one traverses such deep trials alone. Even once lost, we are never forsaken.

Now, sufficiently oriented, let us dive fully into the tale before us! Farrah awaits, as does the flickering hope she will nurture inside despite gusting winds. Walk with me - I promise you illumination awaits within these pages.

Farrah

A kind-hearted young fairy who delights in playing tricks and bringing laughter to her village. She loses her inner light and falls into a deep depression, feeling alone and hopeless. Farrah goes on a transformative journey to rekindle her spirit with the help of trusted friends and a wise mentor. She emerges with a renewed sense of purpose - to help guide others out of darkness.

Farrah was always a joyful and lighthearted fairy who loved bringing laughter to her village through harmless pranks and jokes. She had a core group of loyal friends like Willa who appreciated her gifts of humor and creativity.

In her late teens, Farrah started feeling pressure from some in the community to settle down and conform to more traditional fairy roles and hobbies. She began questioning if her playful spirit was just childish folly. Self-doubt took root and chipped away at Farrah's naturally vibrant personality over time.

When Farrah's father - her biggest cheerleader - passed away one harsh winter, it sent her reeling emotionally. She slowly withdrew from friends and activities as depression and anxiety consumed her. Farrah's dramatic dimming puzzled those close to her who remembered her lively spirit.

Willa

Farrah's lifelong best friend. A loyal pixie with a compassionate spirit. She stays steadfastly by Farrah's side through her deepest despair, never giving up hope. Willa helps Farrah gradually rebuild through her unwavering love and patient encouragement. Her friendship is a lifeline through Farrah's darkest times.

Willa and Farrah bonded instantly as young pixies in fairy school, both feeling they were "different feathers" than their peers. While Willa was shyer, she was drawn to Farrah's bold humour and creativity. They balanced each other beautifully for years.

As Farrah withdrew when the depression hit, Willa remained loyal and concerned. Having grown up feeling like an outsider herself, Willa was sensitive to mental health struggles. She made it her unwavering mission to stand by Farrah when she stopped believing in herself.

Edgar

A thoughtful elf and another of Farrah's trusted friends. He tries doggedly to lift Farrah's spirits when she first spirals into gloom. Edgar never abandons Farrah, always remaining a kind, helpful presence during her recovery back into light. His companionship and care are integral to Farrah's emerging whole again.

Edgar always admired Farrah's talent for spreading laughter and joy effortlessly to all those around her. They developed an easy, affectionate friendship built on good-hearted banter over the years.

When Farrah spiralled into isolation, Edgar felt helpless at first. He responded by constantly showing up with offers of support, wanting to understand her struggle and show he wasn't going anywhere. His quiet belief in Farrah played a key role in her recovery.

Maya

A cheery young pixie with boundless energy and enthusiasm. Her sunny spirit often helps temporarily brighten Farrah's mood even during bleak periods. Maya reminds Farrah of the simple joys of childhood play and imagination. She buoyantly cheers Farrah's gradual return to her true self.

Ignitus

A great ancient phoenix who becomes Farrah's mentor. With empathy born of his own hardships, Ignitus teaches Farrah that her inner light and happiness will return in time if she can survive the darkest nights. His wisdom and compassion leave an indelible mark on Farrah, inspiring her future purpose.

In his youth, Ignitus was a fierce warrior phoenix, ruthless in battle and arrogant. After a tragedy causes him deep remorse, he isolates himself in grief for years before a healer helps him see hope again.

Ignitus emerges renewed with a desire to share his hard-won wisdom on resilience and inner light with lost souls battling darkness. His patience, empathy and guidance act like a lighthouse leading many back to shore from stormy seas.

Chapter 1: Laughter Lost

Farrah zipped playfully through the forest, her translucent wings fluttering rapidly. She giggled as she swooped and dove between the colourful autumn trees, leaving a trail of glittering pixie dust in her wake. Up ahead, she spotted her target - her best friend Willa perched on a toadstool, brushing her violet hair.

"Perfect target," Farrah whispered to herself, suppressing another giggle. She stealthily plucked a vibrant blue flower from a nearby bush. Holding the bloom behind her back, she silently glided up behind her unsuspecting friend, Willa.

"Boo!" Farrah shouted.

Willa shrieked and whirled around in shock. Realizing it was just Farrah's prank, she clutched her chest and exhaled dramatically.

"Farrah! You about scared the sparkles right out of me!" she exclaimed.

Giggling uncontrollably, Farrah presented the bright blue blossom with an exaggerated flourish. "Gotcha again!"

Despite her annoyance, Willa couldn't help but smile, accepting the peace offering. She was used to her best friend's impish tricks. Seeing Farrah's eyes alight with laughter made all her antics worth it.

This was one of Farrah's favourite activities - playing harmless pranks and bringing laughter to her fellow magical creatures. There was no better sound to her than the tinkling laugh of a pixie or the rumbling chortle of a troll. Farrah relished every smile or chuckle she coaxed out of someone with her antics. As she darted away to find her next target, Farrah felt pure giddy exhilaration course through her. What could be better than spreading playful magic through the forest?

"Did you see how high Willa jumped?" Farrah asked a nearby squirrel. "I thought she was going to rocket right off that mushroom!"

The squirrel chittered with amusement. Farrah gave it a wink, then zoomed off to find her next target. Who would it be today? She scanned the forest below, considering her options. Perhaps she could toss acorns at Edgar the elf as he gathered potion ingredients, or leave a trail of glitter leading the wrong way on a signpost. The possibilities for fun and laughter were endless!

As Farrah flew, she spread her arms wide and took a deep breath of the fresh forest air. She loved this time of year, when the leaves were a kaleidoscope of colours and the air had a crisp bite signalling the approach of autumn. The other fairies were gathering nuts and seeds to store for winter, but Farrah wasn't worried about that yet. She was simply focused on enjoying the present and bringing cheer to everyone she could.

Down below, Farrah spied a group of pixies having a picnic. She quietly gathered up some colourful leaves and then floated up right above them.

"Incoming!" she yelled playfully, as she tossed handfuls of leaves over them like confetti. The pixies looked up in surprise, then dissolved into giggles when they saw who it was.

"Good one, Farrah!" Dessa the pixie called up to her. The others waved happily.

Farrah bowed with exaggerated flair. "Thank you, thank you! Just spreading the joy!" She blew them kisses as she zipped away.

Nearby, she noticed a baby phoenix learning to fly for the first time. His wings wobbled uncertainly as he took off from his nest. Farrah quickly flew underneath him.

"I've got you, don't worry!" she reassured the anxious fledgling. Slowly and steadily, she provided support from below until he was able to stabilize himself in the air.

"I did it, I did it!" he cheered once he was successfully airborne.

"You sure did!" Farrah gave him a gentle high-five. She loved nurturing that sense of accomplishment and confidence in young creatures.

Twirling gleefully, Farrah scanned the woods below until she spotted Edgar, hard at work gathering potion ingredients. An impish plot already brewing, she silently gathered a pile of acorns and took aim.

"Incoming!" Farrah yelled as she pelted Edgar with the acorns, sputtering with laughter at his confusion.

Soon, the elf was laughing too and trying to return fire. Farrah easily evaded him with her quick wings, blowing him a teasing kiss as she zipped out of range.

With a contented sigh, she soared above the forest canopy, spreading her arms wide to embrace the crisp autumn breeze. Looking down at the kaleidoscope of ruby, amber and emerald leaves filled her heart with awe. She lived for this time of year, with its fresh earthy scents and sense of cosy nostalgia.

Farrah released the worries of winter yet to come, simply relishing the present. She wanted everyone she encountered to feel that same light-hearted joy and wonder too.

As the sun began to set, Farrah decided it was time to return home. She twirled gleefully through the darkening forest, reflecting on all the smiles she'd helped create today. When she spread joy, she felt it within herself too. What a magical thing laughter was!

Humming contentedly, Farrah fluttered into her tear-shaped pixie home, which was nestled in a towering maple tree overlooking the forest. She was greeted by her pet ladybug, Spot, who flitted in happy circles around her head.

"Hello, Spot!" Farrah giggled. "Your antennae are tickling me."

She gathered some crystallized flower nectar and fed it to the ladybug from her palm. As she did, she recounted the day's highlights.

Farrah sank contentedly into her bed nook piled high with flower petals. She recounted the day's highlights in vivid detail, eyes shining. "Oh Spot, it was such a fun day! Did you see how high Willa jumped when I surprised her? And the baby phoenix flying for the first time? His little wings were flapping so hard!"

Spot wiggled her antennae as she listened to Farrah's stories. The ladybug didn't understand the words, but Farrah's joyful tone said it all.

"Oh Spot, today was magical," Farrah sighed as she drifted off to sleep, a smile still lingering on her lips. In her dreams, she soared through the forest spreading laughter and joy to all she encountered.

After feeding Spot, Farrah curled up in her bed and fell asleep with a smile still lingering on her lips, already dreaming up tomorrow's pranks and jokes. Spot nuzzled against Farrah's hand as she stroked the smooth shiny shell. A contented smile lingered on the fairy's lips as she drifted off, already dreaming up more mischief for tomorrow. The last thought that floated through her mind before sleep's embrace whisked her away was a simple truth that lived inside her spirit - that laughter was the most magical thing in the whole world.

A few weeks later, Farrah once again awoke in her cosy home to the muted morning light filtering through the maple leaves.

7

But she didn't bound out of bed bubbling with excitement like she usually did. Instead, she felt a heavy inertia pinning her wings and limbs down. She lay there gazing up at the dark veins running through the leaves above her, not fully awake but not sleeping either.

Eventually, she sighed and floated slowly out of bed. Even flying seemed to take more effort today for some reason. She pushed open the doors woven from blades of grass and blinked up at the clear blue sky, squinting at the brightness.

Spot buzzed a cheerful greeting around her head. "Not now, Spot," Farrah muttered. The ladybug seemed confused by her owner's dull tone and kept circling her hopefully.

Farrah managed a weak smile. "It's okay, I'm just a little tired today," she assured the pet. "Maybe some breakfast will help."

But inside, Farrah didn't believe her own words. She felt utterly devoid of appetite or motivation. Even the thought of her favourite sugary flower nectar seemed unappetizing. With no idea why, a bleak haze had settled over her, obscuring everything that usually brought her joy.

She went to her pantry nook and nibbled half-heartedly on some crystallized flower nectar. But the sugary treat that normally energized her now seemed to turn to cardboard in her mouth. After a few bites, she gave up and shoved the rest away in defeat.

As she listlessly stared out her window, Farrah spotted a few pixies whispering to each other and looking in her direction. She sighed. Her friends were probably waiting for her to come out and entertain them like usual. But for some reason, the thought of playing pranks or telling jokes today felt just as unappetizing as breakfast had.

"Sorry friends, I don't think I'm up for fun today," Farrah murmured under her breath, even though she knew the pixies couldn't hear her through the glass. Part of her desperately wanted to rush outside and pretend everything was alright. But the bleak fog smothering her thoughts pinned her in place. She was trapped.

Overwhelmed by the sudden inexplicable gloom clutching her heart, Farrah sank down onto her bed and buried her weary head in her hands. What was wrong with her? She felt so numb and heavy like all the light had suddenly been snuffed out from the world. She had no energy or appetite and nothing seemed interesting anymore. It was such a strange feeling.

Gentle pressure against her knee made Farrah peek up to see Spot nudging against her, antennae drooping with concern in her black eyes. Farrah managed a sad smile. Farrah stroked the ladybug's shiny shell absent-mindedly, taking comfort in the soothing texture.

"I'll be okay, Spot," she said, trying to sound reassuring. "Just need to take it easy today. I'm sure I'll be back to normal tomorrow." But inside, Farrah had never felt more lost and hopeless. This impenetrable fog smothering her spirit was utterly foreign and she had no idea how to make it lift again.

Blinking back sudden tears, Farrah curled into a ball atop her flower petal bed, wishing with all her heart she could just disappear until this awful gloom passed. But try as she may to hide, an insidious voice inside told her this dark feeling was her new reality and she may never escape its paralyzing grip.

But when tomorrow came, Farrah felt no different. If anything, the exhaustion and lack of motivation were even more pronounced. The weak sunlight spilling across her face mocked her, underscoring the bleak haze thickening in her mind. She lay in bed long after she normally would have risen, staring up at the underside of leaves to avoid facing the world outside these walls that suddenly felt so daunting.

She knew she should get up and eat, but the thought of expending energy on any task felt overwhelming. Even floating around seemed like entirely too much work. As she lay there, tears welled up unexpectedly and spilled down her cheeks.

"What's wrong with me, Spot?" she whispered, as the ladybug nuzzled against her arm. Farrah gently stroked Spot's antennae for comfort. She wished she knew how to make herself feel better.

But she imagined the concern on her friends' faces if she hid away again and reluctantly dragged herself up. Even floating the few steps to her basin took monumental effort today. Farrah splashed the cold water on her face, but its refreshing tingle was only fleeting.

Later that day, there was a tentative knock against her wooden door. "Farrah?" came Willa's muffled but cheery voice."We're all going fruit picking later! I know how much you love blackberry tarts. Want to come?"

Farrah grimaced, her stomach twisted anxiously. Normally the thought of gorging on ripe blackberries would tempt her greatly, but right now the thought of forcing cheerful small talk all afternoon made her feel ill. She remained silent, hoping Willa would think she was out.

But the pixie knocked again, more insistently. "Farrah? Are you home? We've hardly seen you the past couple of days."

Farrah sighed. It seemed Willa wasn't going to let this go.

"Sorry, not today," she finally answered weakly, knowing how puzzled and hurt Willa must be by her continual refusals.

"Oh, okay…" Willa sounded disappointed but still gentle. "Well, want us to bring you back some blackberries later?"

The offer was kind, but Farrah cringed internally. She didn't want to have to force a smile and pretend to be excited. She just wanted to be left alone.

"No, I'm alright. Thanks though," she replied, grimacing at the lie.

After an awkward pause, Willa responded "Okay, well feel better!" Farrah listened to the sound of her friend's wings fluttering away.

She knew the pixies meant well, but she wished they would stop asking her to do things. She could barely get through the day as it was without any additional tasks or pressures. Right now, just making it to tomorrow felt like enough of a challenge.

Farrah sank back down onto her rumpled bed, berating herself. Why did she keep pushing away those trying to help? But the thought of venturing out and pretending everything was fine felt unbearable. She was trapped in this bleak fog and there didn't seem any way out.

Maybe if she just waited here long enough, asleep or staring blankly at nothing, this awful heaviness would finally lift again. But deep down, Farrah suspected this time the darkness was here to stay. All she could do was close her eyes and pray for numb oblivion to claim her.

As the days crawled by in a featureless haze, Farrah withdrew further into her home, she would drift in and out of fitful sleep, or else gaze listlessly out her window as the world outside passed by without her. She lost all concept of time, the hours bleeding into one another endlessly.

When exhaustion finally overtook her, she would collapse into bed. But true rest eluded her most nights. Farrah would stare up at the darkened leaves above her bed for hours, thoughts churning anxiously or else completely blank.

She only dragged herself up when thirst or hunger eventually overpowered the oppressive inertia pinning her beneath the covers. But no food tempted her palette anymore. The once sugary sweet flower nectar now tasted of cardboard in her mouth after a bite or two. Even personal hygiene began to slip - she couldn't recall her last bath or when she had last combed her hair.

Spot the ladybug faithfully stayed by her side the whole time. Though Farrah had little energy to play with the pet, her presence still provided some small measure of comfort.

Farrah's friends continued trying to lure her out with invitations, but she declined them all, the very thought of pretending to smile or make lighthearted chatter filling her with dread. It was easier to hide than see their worried disappointment. After a while, the invitations tapered off, leaving only an occasional concerned knock on the door. Farrah knew her isolation worried them, but she couldn't bring herself to pretend everything was okay. It was easier to simply hide away.

Inside, Farrah felt swallowed up by a heavy fog that obscured everything she used to enjoy. No matter how much she knew rationally that she should get up and see friends or do activities, she couldn't push through the haze. It was as if all the sparkle had seeped out of her world, leaving everything dim, grey and devoid of meaning.

She wasn't sure how to explain these foreign feelings. All she knew was that the sadness clung to her heavily and wouldn't let go no matter how much she wished it would.

So, Farrah simply waited, in numb limbo for something nameless and impossible - for this unbearable greyness clouding her mind to let go of its grip, for laughter and colour to miraculously return to her muted world. She moved through the days in a dull haze and wished she could feel normal again. She longed for her old lightness and laughter to cut through this smothering fog that had settled upon her. But no matter how she strained for it, that joy continued to feel very far away.

Each moment felt like wading through thick mud, hopeless and drained. She watched leaves blowing in the wind outside and ached to feel that same weightless freedom once more. But it continued to elude her, just out of reach.

One morning, Farrah heard an insistent tapping against her door. She slowly opened her eyes, blinking against the sunlight streaming in through the window.

"Farrah! It's Willa. Please let me in," her friend pleaded from outside.

Farrah grimaced. She didn't want company, but Willa's voice held a note of urgency that was hard to ignore. With a sigh, Farrah dragged herself out of bed and shuffled over to unlatch the door.

Willa burst in, her wings buzzing anxiously. "Oh, thank goodness! We've all been so worried about you, love. Are you ill?"

Farrah shrugged listlessly. "I'm not sick exactly. Just tired."

Willa's eyes widened as she took in Farrah's unkempt appearance and sullen demeanour. This was so unlike the normally vibrant, mischievous fairy.

"Why don't you come out with us today?" Willa suggested gently. "It's a lovely sunny day, perfect for collecting acorns. That always cheers you up."

Farrah shook her head. "I can't. I just want to be alone."

"But it's been weeks!" Willa protested. She lowered her voice like she was sharing a secret. "We miss your tricks and jokes. No one makes us laugh like you, Farrah."

A ghost of a smile flickered across Farrah's face. She appreciated her friend's efforts to help. But the thought of forcing cheerfulness still felt intolerable.

"I'm sorry, Willa. I'm just not myself lately," she tried to explain. "Everything feels...foggy. Like I'm trying to fly through clouds."

Willa's face fell. She hated seeing the usual light in Farrah's eyes dimmed to a flat grey.

"I wish I knew how to help. Will you at least try to eat something?" she pleaded.

Farrah looked down at the crystallised nectar sitting untouched in her pantry. She hadn't been able to stomach more than a few bites a day for weeks now. But she nodded, not wanting to worry Willa more.

"Alright. I'll try," she acquiesced.

Seeming relieved, Willa stepped forward to give Farrah a gentle hug. "Look after yourself. And remember we all care about you very much."

After Willa left, Farrah picked listlessly at the nectar. But even the sweet taste she normally loved turned to sawdust in her mouth after a few bites. Defeated, she crawled back under the covers, feeling even more hopeless after Willa's visit.

Farrah wished she could be the fairy she used to be, but she didn't know how to find her way through this gloomy fog suffocating her spirit. All she could do was close her eyes and pray she would someday wake up feeling like herself again.

A few more days crawled by. Farrah passed the time sleeping fitfully or staring blankly out her window at the forest leaves whisking by in the wind. How she wished she could feel that breezy, free sensation again.

One morning, the sound of young pixies playing outside playing a game of hide-and-seek wafted up through Farrah's open. Their infectious giggles and shouts pierced Farrah's fog-like rays of light. She realized how much she missed bringing that kind of joy to others.

Impulsively, Farrah dragged her leaden body upright and slowly pulled herself out of bed. She had to consciously force each step across her cottage to peer outside. The vibrant autumn leaves and bright sunlight contrasted mockingly with her inner dimness. But seeing the pixies' smiles sparked some faint ember of motivation within her.

She grimaced at her reflection in a looking glass - limp hair, rumpled dress and dim eyes. After the long isolation, she barely recognized herself anymore. Moving reluctantly as though submerged in water, Farrah slowly splashed some water from a basin on her face and then neatly combed her blonde locks and dressed herself for the first time in days. But with great effort, she neatened her appearance as best she could which made her feel a bit more fairy-like.

Just leaving her cottage would require all her strength today, with that Farrah took a deep breath, then ventured outside for the first time in weeks. She winced against the bright sunlight. Gradually her eyes adjusted, taking in the vibrant reds and golds of the autumn leaves.

One of the young pixies, Maya, noticed her emergence and zoomed over. You came!" the energetic pixie exclaimed, grabbing Farrah's hand to lead her towards the others before she could protest. Farrah flinched, overwhelmed by the sudden influx of sights, smells and noises after so long spent in silence. But she forced herself to stay rooted in place.

The pixies crowded eagerly around her, chattering excitedly about how much they missed her antics and tricks Farrah managed a weak smile, though inside she remained numb and anxious. "Hi, Maya. I heard you playing and thought I'd come to say hello." Being immersed in the energy of the group felt utterly foreign after the inertia of her depression.

17

Maya beamed and took Farrah's hand, leading her towards the others. "We're so happy you're here! Come play hide-and-seek with us."

The other pixies crowded around Farrah, chattering excitedly. She felt simultaneously warmed by their enthusiasm and overwhelmed by the sudden social interaction.

"I...I'm not sure I'm up for playing today," Farrah stammered, backing away. The pixies' faces fell.

"Oh, okay," Maya said, sounding disappointed. "Will you at least come have lunch with us?"

Farrah hesitated. The thought of pretending to be cheerful through a whole meal felt draining. But she saw the hopeful looks trained on her and felt guilty.

"Alright, just for a little while," she acquiesced. The pixies cheered and pulled her towards their picnic.

Sensing her discomfort, the others gave Farrah some space while continuously trying to entice her into conversation and activity. As the young ones babbled around her, Farrah picked at a muffin, managing a few small bites. She appreciated her friends' efforts to include her, even though she still felt detached and anxious.

After the brief but exhausting social interaction, when the pixies flitted off to play, Farrah snuck quietly back inside her home, feeling simultaneously guilty and relieved. She knew her friends were only trying to lift her spirits with inclusion and cheer. But right now, she could barely lift herself. She leaned against the sturdy closed door, feeling utterly spent from the social interaction. The brief outing had drained what paltry reserves of energy she had, but it was a small step. Like trying to fly through dense fog, she just had to keep forcing herself into uncomfortable new airspace and have faith that she would eventually break through. Maybe one day, the darkness would lift again. Until then, there was nowhere to go but forward into the unknown, inch by inch. As she laid down to rest her weary mind, she wished she could feel like her true self again. The darkness still clung to her like a wet cloak, making everything a struggle.

Spot nuzzled against her, seeming to sense her sadness. Farrah stroked the ladybug gently. At least one creature's affection came without pressure or judgment.

"Thank you for sticking by me," Farrah whispered. Curled up with Spot, she finally managed to fall into a deep, dreamless sleep.

The next day, Farrah awoke feeling just as weary and lifeless as before her brief outing the previous day. The heavy gloom settled onto her again like a wet cloak. She considered lying in bed, watching dust motes drift through the pale morning light. hiding from the world outside that seemed so dauntingly bright and lively compared to her inner dimness.

There was a tentative knock at the door. "Farrah?" Willa's gentle voice called. "I've brought you some chamomile tea and scones. May I come in?"

Farrah grimaced. She appreciated Willa checking on her but didn't feel up to more company. Still, she knew her friend meant well.

"Come in," Farrah replied weakly.

Willa entered holding a tray, which she set down on the pantry shelf. Her wings drooped slightly when she saw Farrah still in bed.

"Oh dear, you're not feeling any better, are you love?" Willa asked.

Farrah shook her head, tears stinging her eyes. "No. I don't know what's wrong with me. It's like I'm trapped in this gloomy fog."

Willa sat down on the edge of the flower petal bed. "I wish I could make it all better. But the best I can do is bring you tea and lend an ear if you need to talk."

Farrah managed a faint smile. "I appreciate that. Thank you for still being my friend, even when I'm poor company."

"Of course! We just want you back to your old cheerful self," said Willa. She stood up reluctantly. "I should let you rest. But if you need anything at all, we're right outside."

After Willa left, Farrah sipped the chamomile tea. Its warmth did seem to ever-so-slightly lift the chill that had settled into her bones. She nibbled the edge of a scone, though it still tasted like cardboard.

Later, she stood at the window, watching the pixies play tag amidst the falling leaves. Their high-pitched laughter echoed up to her. Farrah closed her eyes, aching to feel that kind of giddy joy again.

But for now, all she could do was wrap her arms around herself against the loneliness and wait. She hoped time would eventually carry her out of this bleak fog - but the waiting felt endless.

"Please come back to me," she whispered into the grey emptiness. But only silence answered.

The next morning, Farrah awoke feeling empty and listless as always. She stared up at the leaves above her bed, following the veins as if they might provide some answers. But of course, they held no solutions to the dark fog smothering her spirit.

With a sigh, Farrah rose and shuffled to her wash basin. As she splashed the cold water on her face, she caught a glimpse of her reflection. Dull eyes stared back, framed by limp blonde hair. Farrah turned away, discouraged by the complete lack of light or joy visible in her features.

A knock at the door startled her. "Farrah? It's Edgar."

Farrah grimaced. Edgar the elf was another of her concerned

friends attempting to lift her spirits. While part of her appreciated their efforts, the rest of her wished to avoid the pressure of social interaction. But she knew Edgar would not be deterred easily.

Reluctantly, she opened the door. Edgar's eyes widened when he saw her dishevelled state.

"Oh, Farrah..." he said sympathetically. "We've all been so worried about you. Please, tell me how I can help."

Farrah shook her head. "I don't think anyone can help. I just feel...numb. Like I'm trapped in a dark forest, searching for a light to lead me out."

Edgar stepped forward and put a comforting hand on her shoulder. "You don't have to face this alone, my friend. Let us guide you through the darkness. We can search for the light together."

Looking into Edgar's kind, earnest eyes, Farrah felt her resolve weaken. Perhaps it was time to stop hiding away. If her friends could lend their light to hers, together they might illuminate a way forward.

"Alright," she acquiesced wearily. "I'll try to let you all in. But it's not easy when everything feels so gloomy."

"I know," Edgar said sympathetically. "But we're here for you, one step at a time."

He coaxed her outside to sit in the sunshine among the bustling pixies. Though she still felt detached and anxious, for the first time Farrah allowed a flicker of hope to glow inside. With help, perhaps she could find her way out of this darkness after all.

The warmth of the midday sun on her skin felt soothing, like a gentle hug warming her from the outside in. Farrah sat quietly, watching the pixies laugh and play. Though their cheerfulness still felt out of reach for her own mood, she appreciated their bright spirits.

After a while, Edgar brought over two steaming mugs. "I made us some elderflower tea," he said, handing Farrah a cup.

She managed a faint smile. "Thank you."

They sipped their tea in companionable silence. The earthy, floral taste did seem to ground Farrah, making her feel a bit more present and connected to the living forest around her.

"How are you feeling today?" Edgar asked gently after a few minutes.

Farrah stared down into the dregs of her tea. "A little better, I think. Being outside helps, as does everyone's company."

She knew that admitting that small bit of progress was important. If she kept pretending, she wanted to be alone, her friends would have no choice but to respect that.

Edgar's face lit up. "I'm so glad. We want you to know we're here whenever you're ready for togetherness or talk."

Farrah nodded, thankful for his compassion. She still felt the heavy fog clinging to her, but the tea and conversation were small rays of light cutting through the gloom.

Later, when she went back inside to rest, Farrah decided to leave the window open. She closed her eyes and listened to the pixies' infectious laughter drifting in. Though she was still struggling, opening herself up to loved ones was the first step toward finding her way out of the darkness.

The next morning, Farrah awoke feeling a bit more rested than usual. A ray of sunshine was streaming in through her open window, illuminating the dust motes dancing through the air.

As she floated slowly out of bed, Farrah decided she would try to do more than just sit outside today. If she kept staying within her comfort zone, she may never have pushed through the fog that still lingered in her mind.

After eating some breakfast, Farrah took a deep breath and left her house. The sunlight immediately warmed her wings, filling her with a bit more motivation. She saw Edgar and Willa chatting nearby and approached them.

"Good morning," she greeted them, trying to sound upbeat. "How are you both today?"

"We're wonderful now that you're here!" Willa exclaimed, giving Farrah a gentle hug. "You're looking a bit brighter today."

Farrah nodded. "I'm feeling a little better. I was wondering if I could join you in gathering potion ingredients today?"

"Of course!" Edgar replied merrily. "We'd love your company."

Farrah felt a nervous flutter in her stomach. Part of her just wanted to retreat back home where it felt safe. But she knew if she avoided the challenge, she may stay trapped indefinitely in the gloom.

So, she ventured into the forest with her friends, searching for berries and mushrooms. Though she moved slower than usual and spoke little, the sunshine and fresh air gradually reinvigorated her. Farrah realized she had almost forgotten the feel of soil beneath her feet and the wind in her hair.

That evening after returning home, Farrah blinked with surprise to see her basket full of colourful ingredients. Despite the lingering fog, she had still managed to gather plants and complete a task. A tiny ember of pride flickered within her at this small accomplishment.

As she lay down to sleep, Farrah felt the first faint stirrings of belief that just maybe, one slow step at a time, she could find her way out of the darkness after all.

The next few days brought a mix of light and shadow. While Farrah still struggled with motivation on her low days, she tried to hold onto the progress she had made.

On a morning when she awoke feeling weighed down and

lethargic, Farrah considered staying in bed rather than facing the day. But she thought of how disappointed her friends would be and managed to reluctantly get up and dressed.

Pushing open her creaky front door, she forced herself to take unsteady steps outside. The sunlight stung her eyes, amplifying the headache buzzing behind her temples.

Maya spotted her immediately and zoomed over, grinning ear to ear. "Farrah! We're playing hide and seek, come join!"

Before Farrah could object, the persistent pixie grabbed her hand and tugged her towards the others gathered around a large oak tree base. Maya began enthusiastically explaining the rules while Farrah stood numbly.

She knew she should gently excuse herself to avoid another exhausting round of false cheer. But the hopeful faces surrounding her made Farrah feel guilty at the thought of disappointing them again.

Farrah grimaced slightly. The thought of running around yelling right now made her head pound more. But she also knew isolating herself again could undo all her recent progress.

"Alright, just one game," she acquiesced hoarsely. As Maya and the others scurried off to hide giggling, their shouts amplified the ache pounding behind Farrah's temples. But seeing their smiles peeking out occasionally sparked some faint light inside her darkness.

Trying her best to ignore her throbbing head, Farrah played along as the pixies noisily darted off to hide. Their giggles and shouts echoed sharply in her skull. But when she saw their smiling faces peeking out from bushes and tree hollows, she felt a flicker of levity.

At least she had gotten outside today, Farrah reassured herself. After the game concluded, Farrah retreated to sit alone under a shady oak. Away from the chaos, she began to feel a bit better. And she realized that even on bad days, showing up could help maintain the upward trajectory. Progress was not linear, but any step forward was still important. With time, she prayed the darkness imprisoning her might relent its clutches.

That night, curled up with Spot, Farrah felt the softness of the pet's shell and allowed it to soothe her. Though depression still visited her frequently, she was slowly learning strategies to avoid slipping back into isolation. She gave Spot an extra snuggle, thankful for the unconditional support.

The next morning, Farrah awoke with a feeling of determination. Today would be the day she tried to spread her wings fully again.

She floated outside, greeted by golden beams of sunlight streaming through the trees. Taking a deep breath, Farrah began flapping her shimmering wings faster and faster until her feet lifted off the ground. Though she wobbled at first, soon she was zipping smoothly through the brisk autumn air.

Farrah allowed herself to get lost in the feeling of the wind

27

rushing against her face. She did loops, dives and twirls, revelling in the freedom of motion. Flying used to be second nature, but now it felt exhilarating.

Maya and her friends looked up and began cheering Farrah on as she swooped by. Buoyed by their support, Farrah soared up above the treetops, bursting through the canopy into dazzling sunlight.

Giggling giddily, she paused to hover in midair and take in the breathtaking view. The forest spread out below her like a rippling emerald sea. Farrah felt connected once more to the beauty around her.

As she descended back into the shelter of leaves, Farrah realized she had truly escaped the fog today. While she knew gloomy days still lay ahead, her spirit felt illuminated from within.

Landing gracefully among her friends, Farrah saw their beaming smiles and outstretched arms. She felt as though she was seeing the world clearly for the first time in forever. After so many bleak days, she had emerged from the darkness.

"Welcome back, Farrah," Willa whispered, embracing her friend tightly. "We've missed your light."

Chapter 2: An Impenetrable Fog Descends

Farrah glided slowly through the forest, pausing to touch the leaves that were morphing from green to rich shades of amber and ruby. Autumn was in full swing now. She smiled as a chestnut dropped from an overhead branch right into her outstretched palm.

Her reemergence back into the world after days of isolation had felt miraculous. But as the days wore on, that familiar heaviness and gloom began creeping back in at the edges like gnarled fingers grasping at her wings.

She could feel the dark fog trying to reclaim her, even as she fought to stay present. Farrah pressed on through the forest, determined not to relinquish the progress she'd made. She focused on the feel of the cold earth beneath her feet and the freshness of the air in her lungs.

Up ahead, Edgar waved cheerfully from beneath a dogwood tree. "Hello, Farrah! Lovely day for a stroll."

Farrah attempted a smile. "Yes, it's nice to get out." She struggled to think of more to say, to have even a small conversation. But the words dried up in her throat.

An uncomfortable silence hung between them for a few beats. Farrah felt irrationally annoyed with Edgar for highlighting her difficulty with basic social interactions lately.

"Well, don't let me keep you," she mumbled awkwardly. "I

should get back home."

Farrah gave Edgar a quick wave before turning and fluttering away, berating herself. Why was even a simple chat so taxing nowadays? She had been able to fly effortlessly through forests and spread cheer with ease her whole life. Now even a walk left her depleted.

Back home, Farrah collapsed into her bed nook and closed her eyes. But exhaustion eluded her. The interaction with Edgar kept replaying in her mind, an endless loop of self-criticism.

A knock at the door jolted her upright. "Farrah?" Willa's voice called. "Can I come in?"

Farrah scowled. Couldn't she just be left alone? But she knew Willa would not be deterred so easily. With a sigh, she hauled herself up and opened the door.

Willa's eyes filled with concern when she saw the state Farrah was in. "Oh, love. Are you not feeling well again?"

Farrah shrugged listlessly. "I'm fine. Just tired."

"Did something happen?" Willa pressed gently. "You seemed a bit happier the last few days. I thought the worst was behind you."

Irritation pricked at Farrah. Why couldn't everyone stop scrutinizing her mood?

"Well, it's not," she snapped. Seeing Willa's hurt expression, Farrah's face softened. "I'm sorry. I just can't keep pretending I'm okay when I'm not."

Willa reached out and took Farrah's hand, giving it a supportive squeeze. "You don't have to pretend. And you don't have to go through this alone. We all just want to help."

Looking into Willa's kind, earnest eyes, Farrah felt her frustration dissipate. Her friends were only trying to support her. Perhaps it was time to stop pushing them away again.

"You're right," she said quietly. "I know you only want to help. It's just...hard."

Willa nodded sympathetically. "I can't imagine. But we're here for you. Why don't you come over for tea later? Just a quiet visit."

Farrah managed a faint smile. Tea did sound nice. "Alright. I'll come by soon."

After Willa left, Farrah stood at her window watching the leaves swirl down in the wind. She placed her hand on the glass, taking comfort in its cool solidity. Though the gloom still lingered at the corners of her mind, she focused on keeping it at bay through simple sensory details - the smooth glass beneath her fingertips, the earthy scent of the autumn air. For this moment at least, she kept the darkness pushed back by clinging to what was real.

Later that day, Farrah forced herself to visit Willa as planned. She had to constantly resist the urge to make an excuse and hide away in bed instead. But she managed to follow through, arriving at Willa's cosy hollow of a home just as the sun was setting.

"Farrah! So glad you could make it," Willa welcomed her warmly. She ushered her inside, where a kettle was already steaming over a small fire.

The two friends sat together sipping chamomile tea and watching the flames dance. Willa kept the conversation light, chatting about the changing weather and amusing forest gossip. Farrah mostly listened, soaking up the comforting atmosphere.

Over the next week, Farrah made an effort to see friends every day, even when it felt like trying to fly through dense fog. She went on nature walks, drank tea and played quiet games of hide-and-seek. Being around loved ones seemed to lift the gloom, if only temporarily. The heaviness always threatening to settle back upon her as soon as she was alone again.

But Farrah kept fighting it as days turned into weeks. She put on an outward show of cheerfulness that became a habit, even as her inner light dimmed. It was easier to fake a smile than to face the fact that despite all her efforts, the darkness was creeping back in.

Soon even pretending to be happy became too taxing. Farrah began declining her friends' invitations with excuses about feeling ill or tired. In truth, she simply didn't have the energy anymore to be around others. Just getting through the day alone felt challenging enough.

Willa, Edgar and the others continued checking on Farrah, but less frequently as it became clear she wanted solitude. Though it pained them to see her withdrawing again, they knew they couldn't force her to accept their help if she wasn't ready.

Alone once more, Farrah retreated fully into her gloom. She passed the days sleeping or staring numbly out her window at the world passing by without her. When she forced herself to get up, it was only to pick at food with no appetite or to sloppily tidy up. Any task felt monumental in her depleted state.

As the weeks wore on, Farrah felt herself being submerged beneath wave after wave of bleakness until she could hardly recall what it felt like to break the surface and breathe freely. The fog had rolled back in thicker than ever and she was adrift in its cold grey infinity once more.

Farrah wasn't sure how long she had been adrift in the gloomy fog. Time seemed to lose all meaning when each day blurred into the next, monotonously bleak. She slept when exhaustion overtook her, though rarely peacefully. Most nights she lay awake watching shadows creep across her wall as the hours stretched endlessly on.

When she couldn't stand the confines of her home any longer, Farrah would force herself outside to wander the forest paths aimlessly. The fresh air should have rejuvenated her, but it only emphasized how disconnected she felt from the living world around her.

One morning when the weight of the fog felt particularly suffocating, Farrah found herself walking to the pixie village on autopilot. She paused at the edge of the cheery commotion, suddenly unsure why she had come.

Maya noticed her lingering under the trees and immediately zoomed over.

"Farrah! It's so good to see you!" she cried. "We've all missed you lately."

Farrah attempted a weak smile. "Hello, Maya. I just...went for a walk." She grasped for an excuse for showing up unannounced.

"Well, I'm glad your walk brought you here," said Maya. "Come sit with us!"

Before Farrah could protest, the exuberant pixie grabbed her hand and pulled her into the centre of the activity. The other pixies crowded around, chattering excitedly. Farrah froze, overwhelmed by the sudden influx of sensory details assaulting her.

Maya babbled on, oblivious to Farrah's distress. "...and then I said, 'But toadstools can't fly!' Wasn't that hilarious?"

Farrah's chest constricted. She needed to escape. Now.

"I…I have to go," she gasped out. Before the pixies could react, she whirled around and took off running back up the forest path. She didn't stop until she was safely back home with the door shut firmly behind her.

Farrah collapsed onto her bed, breathing heavily. Her heart pounded against her ribs like a caged bird. She berated herself for giving in to the impulse to see friends when she clearly wasn't ready.

A soft knock sounded at her door. "Farrah?" came Willa's tentative voice. "Is everything alright? We're worried."

Farrah curled tighter into a ball. "I'm fine," she called out hoarsely. "Just leave me be."

She listened to the sound of Willa's retreating wings fading into the distance. Part of Farrah longed to call out to her friend, to let her know it wasn't her fault. But the words remained trapped in her throat.

Wishing she could just disappear, Farrah finally managed to cry herself into a fitful sleep. No one could understand the storms raging within her. She had to weather this bleak fog on her own.

Over the next few days, Farrah spiraled further into despair. She barely had the energy now to leave her bed, instead staring blankly at the walls for hours without moving. It was as if her inner light had been entirely snuffed out, leaving behind an empty shell.

Her concerned friends came by daily, still knocking gently on her door even when she refused to respond. But their voices barely penetrated the grey fog cocooning Farrah. She knew they cared, but couldn't muster the strength to see them.

One morning, Willa entered without waiting for a reply to her knock. Farrah didn't even stir from the bed as her friend rushed over.

"Oh, Farrah," Willa whispered, seeing the state she was in. Farrah's eyes were sunken and dull and her wings had lost their magical shimmer.

Willa took Farrah's limp hand in both of hers. "Stay here, love. I'm going to make you some tea and soup."

Though the kind gestures barely registered in Farrah's numb mind, a small ember of gratitude flickered deep within. She remained unmoving as Willa bustled quietly around the kitchen.

When Willa returned with the tea and food, Farrah managed to sit up just enough to take a few sips and small bites. The taste was like sawdust in her mouth, but she ate to provide Willa some small reassurance.

"There now, just a little at a time," Willa soothed. "I'll come back to check on you tomorrow." She smoothed Farrah's tangled hair and tucked the blankets around her.

After Willa left, Farrah faded back into detached numbness. But she knew she was lucky to have a friend so persistent in her care. It was a faint lifeline within the still-suffocating gloom.

In the darkest moments over those bleak days, the memory of Willa's compassion became Farrah's only tether. Even when she lacked any will to save herself, knowing others still cared kept her going when she wanted most to just fade away. It was barely enough, but it sustained her.

The days continued to blur together in a haze of grey isolation. Farrah lost track of time, sleeping her days away or staring blankly at nothing. She only roused herself enough to nibble at the food Willa still dutifully brought over, though it all tasted like sawdust.

Willa started coming by twice a day, sitting with Farrah in silence but radiating love and comfort through her presence alone. She tenderly combed Farrah's tangled blonde locks and sang soothing songs in her warbling pixie voice.

One song, about finding light even in the darkest night, made Farrah's eyes well up with tears. Knowing Willa cared so deeply even when she had nothing left to give back stirred some dim flicker inside her hollow heart.

But Farrah remained mute, unable to voice her churning emotions. She hoped Willa could see the gratitude shining in her eyes, even if she could not yet speak it aloud.

After a week of this gentle routine, punctuated only by long hours when Farrah faded into a dreamless sleep, Willa arrived one morning bearing a bouquet of wildflowers.

"Come now, time for some sunshine," Willa said briskly but kindly. When Farrah did not stir, she took her hand and encouraged her up out of bed.

Farrah considered resisting, but Willa's steadfast presence brooked no argument. She allowed herself to be led outside for the first time in days.

The sunlight momentarily blinded her, but soon Farrah began to make out the vibrant blues and yellows of Willa's flowers. Their sweet aroma stirred some long-dormant part of Farrah's spirit.

Willa squeezed her hand supportively. "Baby steps, love. Today we sit in the light. Tomorrow, who knows?"

Farrah managed the ghost of a smile. Willa was right - as long as she kept trying, the fog could not claim her completely. Step by step, she would find her way back.

The next morning, Willa arrived and once again gently encouraged Farrah up and outside. The sunlight seemed slightly less harsh today, the birdsong almost melodic rather than grating.

Willa had brought a hairbrush and patiently worked through Farrah's tangled locks as she hummed a cheery tune. Farrah closed her eyes, focusing on the soothing sensations.

When her hair was smoothed down once more, Farrah ran her fingers over it and turned to Willa. "Thank you," she croaked out in a hoarse whisper. It was the first words she had spoken in days.

Willa's eyes lit up. "Of course, dear!" she exclaimed. "Your voice is the loveliest sound."

Heartened by this small progress, Willa began coaxing Farrah to move about more over the next few days. She walked with Farrah around the meadow, keeping up a steady stream of gentle chatter about flowers and butterflies.

The fresh air and movement seemed to unlock something in Farrah. One day, she paused to cup a perfect blue blossom in her hands, admiring its delicate symmetry.

"It's beautiful," she remarked softly. Willa beamed - it had been so long since Farrah had reacted to anything with wonder.

By the end of the week, Farrah felt strong enough to accompany Willa on short flights around the meadow. Her wings wobbled at first, but soon she was gliding smoothly through the breeze. The fog still clung to the edges of her mind, but for these precious moments, she felt light and free.

That night, curled up in bed, Farrah said a silent prayer of gratitude for her steadfast friend. Recovery was an uphill climb, but Willa made the path less lonely. With her support, Farrah was rediscovering small joys and reminders that beauty still existed all around her.

As the days passed, Farrah could feel her energy and motivation slowly returning thanks to Willa's tireless care. Some mornings the fog still pressed down with suffocating weight, making even getting out of bed feel like trying to push through quicksand.

But Willa would arrive and help guide Farrah gently through the gloom. On darker days they simply sat outside together breathing the fresh air. When she had more energy, they floated leisurely around the meadow or foraged for wild berries.

Bit by bit, Willa encouraged Farrah to engage and open up. After one silent stroll, she turned to her friend and asked tentatively, "How are you feeling today?"

Farrah stared down the forest path. Putting the shapeless despair into words felt challenging. But she focused on a nearby trembling aspen leaf and said quietly, "Like that leaf - barely hanging on."

Willa squeezed her hand. "But it's still there. And so are you."

After that, Willa asked the question daily and each time Farrah found a little more she could express - a heaviness in her chest, a hollowness inside. Voicing even fragments of her despair seemed to lighten it slightly.

Two weeks after her first tentative answer, Farrah responded: "Today is...brighter, I think."

The smile that lit up Willa's face warmed Farrah more than the morning sunbeams streaming through the trees. Her friend's unwavering support was her lifeline.

There were still darker days when the fog rolled back in with crushing weight. But having glimpsed the blue sky again, Farrah found new reserves of strength. She knew now she just had to keep wading through, one step at a time.

With her dear friend beside her, she felt hope flickering inside once more. Together, they would make it through this.

As Farrah's strength slowly returned, Willa began encouraging her to spend time with others besides just herself. One sunny morning, she brought Farrah to the pixie village.

"Come along, Maya and the others can't wait to see you," Willa said gently but firmly.

Farrah hesitated at the village edge. After isolating herself for so long, facing the crowd felt daunting. Sensing her trepidation, Willa gave her hand a reassuring squeeze.

"I'll be right here. One step at a time."

Farrah took a deep breath and allowed Willa to lead her into the bustling square. Immediately they were spotted by Edgar and several young pixies.

"Farrah! So wonderful to see you, friend," Edgar said warmly, giving her shoulder an affectionate pat. The pixies beamed and waved excitedly.

Farrah managed a shaky smile. "Hello everyone. It's nice to be back." She kept her replies minimal, but the genuine delight on her friends' faces touched her deeply.

Overwhelmed after just a short visit, Farrah soon retreated back home to rest. But the next day, Willa coaxed her to come sit with the pixies again during a leisurely breakfast.

Gradually, Farrah grew comfortable with brief interactions once more. A major milestone came several weeks later when she felt up to joining the pixies picking berries in the forest. Moving slowly, she gathered blackberries into her basket, savouring this taste of ordinary life again.

That night, as Farrah lay in bed reflecting, she realized how vital community had been to climbing out of her deep pit of despair. With support, she was blossoming once more - weary and fragile still, but alive again thanks to the unwavering love surrounding her.

As the weeks went on, Farrah continued regaining strength and motivation. She immersed herself in simple activities that connected her to friends and nature - gathering flowers, pressing apples into cider and tending to the community garden.

Focusing on tasks rather than ruminating helped keep the gloom at bay. And the more energy she regained; the lighter Farrah felt. It was a gradual upward climb rather than an overnight transformation, but she celebrated each small step.

On a crisp fall morning, Farrah awoke before sunrise. She floated outside her home, breathing in the bracing pre-dawn air. As the sky lightened, she decided on a whim to visit the meadow on the hill overlooking the pixie village.

Farrah flew swiftly, revelling in the wind whistling against her skin. She broke through the treetops just as the sun crested the horizon, spilling golden light across the meadow grass rippling like waves below.

Perching atop a weathered boulder, Farrah watched in awe as sunrise set the world aglow. The slumbering valley slowly stirred to life under the sun's radiance. Farrah's eyes shone with joyful tears - it had been so long since she'd witnessed this everyday miracle.

When Willa found her still sitting enthralled hours later, Farrah turned to her friend with a beaming smile. "Thank you for showing me beauty again," she said softly.

Willa squeezed her hand, eyes glistening. "The light in you is what we see most beautifully, dear friend."

Farrah knew she still had healing to do. But cocooned in the warmth of friendship and nature's splendour, she felt hope blooming anew. The fog had not claimed her and her inner flame now burned brighter than ever before.

As the weeks went by, Farrah felt herself slowly returning to her old self. She laughed more easily and spread her glittering wings to dance and play with the pixies once again. Bringing joy to friends filled her with a deep satisfaction she had feared was lost forever.

But recovery was not linear and some days the gloom still returned with crushing weight. During those times, Farrah was learning not to be discouraged, but to be gentle with herself. Her friends were always there to provide support until the darkness passed.

One morning when melancholy threatened to overtake her, Farrah woke to find Maya and the pixies gathered outside her door.

"Rise and shine!" Maya called cheerily. "We're taking you somewhere special today."

Farrah managed a faint smile, buoyed as always by their enthusiasm. "Alright, let me get ready."

The pixies led her through the forest to a glen blanketed in vivid wildflowers. "Ta-da!" Maya exclaimed. "We planted them for you, so whenever you're feeling blue, you can come sit among all this beauty."

Farrah's eyes filled with tears. Each blossom was a reminder she was loved. "It's perfect. Thank you all so much."

Encircled by her dearest friends and the flowers they had nurtured for her, Farrah's heart swelled with gratitude. Their kindness helped sustain her through the inevitable dark days.

She knew now that though the fog still wandered at the forest's edge, she had built a glowing sanctuary filled with support and joy to light her way if it threatened to return. With the love surrounding her, she could weather any future storms.

As the weeks went on, Farrah found making art helped process the difficult emotions she was working through. She began collecting fallen leaves, flower petals and twigs, using them to create intricate collages and mosaics. Immersing herself in crafting was meditative and she loved gifting the finished pieces to lift others' spirits too.

On mornings when motivation was scarce, beginning a simple project like weaving a basket or blending botanical inks would provide a sense of purpose and momentum to drive away the malaise. Farrah learned to be gentle with herself on darker days, starting small and building up rather than giving in to frustration.

When she had more creative energy, Farrah worked on larger wood carvings depicting scenes from the enchanted forest. One particularly meaningful project was a sculpture of her friend Willa sitting among wildflowers like the glen the pixies had planted.

Farrah's eyes misted over as she presented it to Willa. "This is to thank you for never giving up on me," she said. "Even when I had lost my way, your friendship guided me through the fog."

Willa wrapped Farrah in a warm embrace. "Your own light shone through, as I knew it would," she whispered. "But your joy multiplies all of ours."

Farrah resolved to focus her magic on spreading that light

through art and community. On difficult days, her friends still rallied around her with compassion and patience. And with each passing season, the fog's hold over her spirit grew a little weaker, replaced by hope.

As spring arrived, breathing new life into the forest, Farrah felt her own rebirth mirroring nature's. She delighted in the carpets of wildflowers unfolding across the meadows and baby animals peeking out from nests and burrows. Each new bud and hatchling was a reminder that darkness gives way to light.

On the first truly warm day, Farrah gathered friends in the sun-dappled glen for a celebratory tea party. Laughter and music floated on the gentle breeze as they feasted on pastries and sipped floral infusions.

When twilight fell, they released a cloud of enchanted fireflies into the air. Farrah and the pixies danced among the swirling lights, leaving shimmering trails of magic in their wake.

Watching her friend twirl blissfully, Willa's heart swelled. Not long ago, they had sat in this same meadow wrapped in gloom. Now Farrah emanated pure joy.

As the fireflies dispersed into the night sky, Farrah pulled Willa into an embrace. "Thank you for seeing light within me, even when I lost sight of it," she said softly.

Willa squeezed her hand. "Your glow was only dimmed for a time. Now it shines brighter than ever."

Farrah knew tomorrow could bring shadows. But anchored by unconditional love, she greeted each day with open arms. Her inner flame had been tested, but burned all the fiercer, lighting her way forward.

As spring gave way to summer, Farrah found solace in her garden. Tending to her flowers and herbs provided a sense of purpose during darker times. Watching the incremental growth and blossoms emerge reminded her that patience and care bear fruit.

On humid days when the fog of malaise threatened to settle in her mind, Farrah would rise early and lose herself in weeding, pruning and planting. Seeing the garden flourish into vibrant life lifted her own spirit.

But Farrah was careful not to overdo it. She was still learning her limits and left time to rest when needed. Her friends gently reminded her not to neglect self-care while pouring energy into such projects.

"The garden is lovely, but we need our fairy most of all," Willa told her one evening after finding Farrah collapsed asleep amid the flower beds.

Farrah smiled wryly. "You're right. What I grow here means little if I'm not taking care of myself too."

From then on, she was diligent about balance - making time for community, reflection and fun alongside tending her garden. Farrah discovered the peace and motivation it brought were amplified when she paced herself.

On evenings when she had the energy to spare, Farrah invited friends to her garden to enjoy the fireflies' glow and feast on just-picked produce. Those nights filled her heart to the brim, surrounded by loved ones beneath the blanket of stars.

Though tainted days still came, her world was alight with renewed possibility. The long nights had taught Farrah to nurture every glimmer persistently - within the soil, within her spirit - trusting it would multiply into boundless beauty.

One sunny morning, Farrah awoke before dawn and floated outside to watch the sunrise. As the inky night sky faded to pastel and gold, her heart swelled with gratitude.

Each new day was a gift after the long darkness she had endured. The light now bathing the meadow seemed more radiant for having been absent for a time.

Farrah lifted her face to the warm beams. In this moment, she felt at complete peace. The fog that had muted her world for so long had finally released its grasp.

She knew there would still be pockets of gloom along the path ahead. But her inner flame was strong again to illuminate the way forward.

Farrah had not conquered the darkness alone. Her friends had kept her tethered to hope when she wanted to give up. Their unwavering love and comfort were the lighthouse that guided her home.

Tears of joy slipped down Farrah's cheeks as she watched the sleeping forest stir to life. Another cycle of the night giving way to dawn, of bleakness shattered by light.

Farrah stretched her shimmering wings and took to the air. She flew over the awakening village, leaves and petals swirling in her wake, smiling faces turning skyward at her radiance.

Dark seasons would come again, but they would pass. Her spirit had been tested and emerged renewed. Now Farrah soared into the sunrise, boldly aglow, to meet the day.

Chapter 3: A Flickering Flame of Hope

Farrah drifted listlessly through the forest undergrowth. The leaves were starting to change from emerald green to shades of amber and ruby, but she barely noticed the beauty around her. An invisible weight pressed down on her shoulders, making even the smallest actions feel like trying to fly through thick mud.

She knew she should try to shake off this melancholy. Only yesterday she had been frolicking with the pixies in the meadow, feeling almost like her old self again. But the gloom had rolled back in overnight, as it always did, dark and inescapable as a thundercloud blocking out the sun.

Farrah wandered aimlessly until the light filtering through the canopy faded to dusk. Finding herself in an unfamiliar part of the woods, she shivered and wrapped her arms around herself. Ever-encroaching shadows leeched what little warmth she had left, leaving her bone-weary.

Farrah sank down at the base of a towering oak tree, head in her hands. All she wanted was to crawl back into the numb oblivion that had cocooned her for weeks. If only she could will away the persistent ache in her spirit.

A dry rasp startled Farrah from her spiral of despair. She peered into the darkness, making out a pair of gleaming golden eyes staring back from a branch overhead. As her vision adjusted, she realized it was a great phoenix, his scarlet plumage muted to burnt umber in the gloaming.

"Forgive my intrusion, but what troubles you, little fairy?" the phoenix inquired, not unkindly. His gravelly voice was soft with age and wisdom.

Farrah tensed. She did not know this creature and was wary of revealing vulnerability. But something in the phoenix's gentle aura told her she could trust him.

"I...I don't know how to explain it," she began hesitantly. "It's like a dark fog descends in my mind sometimes. Obscuring everything that used to bring me joy."

The phoenix nodded sagely. "I understand, child. The soul's seasons change, just as the forest does. There will always be winters - bitter, but temporary."

He fluttered down to land beside Farrah, emitting ethereal warmth that immediately eased her shivering.. Up close, his feathers looked terribly dull and tattered. But his black eyes still held a comforting warmth.

"Walk with me and I will share what I can," he beckoned. Too weary to resist, Farrah rose and followed his graceful stride into the night woods.

"My name is Ignitus," he introduced himself. "I have seen six hundred and seventy-two cycles of the seasons."

Farrah's eyes widened. She could hardly fathom such lifetimes.

Ignitus chuckled. "Surprised I have tottered on this long? Our

55

kind are resilient, though not immune to suffering." A shadow crossed his face.

"You see, I too once lost my inner flame. Two centuries ago, poachers raided my nest, slaying my mate and our hatchlings." His voice broke. "Consumed by rage and grief, I smothered my fire willingly, wanting only oblivion."

Farrah's throat tightened in sympathy. No wonder this phoenix's aura resonated so deeply with her despair.

Ignitus collected himself and continued. "But flames cannot be extinguished forever. Eventually, mine reignited - weakened, but still alight. I lived on, finding purpose again in guiding other wayward souls out of the darkness."

He turned to Farrah. "The longest nights are followed by the dawn if you only hold on till it comes. Take comfort that your fire still smoulders within. With care, it will blaze anew."

Farrah felt the first sparks of hope reigniting in her weary spirit. If this ancient, weathered phoenix could recover his inner light, then perhaps she could rekindle her own in time.

The pair walked on as Farrah opened up about her struggle to stay afloat amidst the gloom that pulled her under for weeks on end. Just voicing the pain out loud seemed to lift it slightly.

By the time Ignitus led her out of the forest back to familiar lands, Farrah felt profoundly grateful for his wisdom and empathy. She had found a flicker of hope to cling to. If she continued trusting those who cared for her, someday the fog would lift for good.

In the days following her encounter with Ignitus, Farrah found her thoughts drifting back to his words of wisdom and comfort. The ancient phoenix's story resonated deeply, kindling her long-dampened hopes that perhaps she too could regain her inner light.

When the gloom descended heavily once more, threatening to crush her fragile spark of optimism, Farrah closed her eyes and recalled Ignitus' gentle voice. "The longest nights are followed by the dawn if you only hold on till it comes."

The mantra soothed her racing mind and allowed her to cling to possibility in her darkest moments. Even a faint glimmer was enough to sustain her for now.

During brief interludes when the fog lifted, Farrah yearned to speak with Ignitus again. His profound understanding would surely help illuminate the ominous maze of her own mind. But finding him in the sprawling forest seemed unlikely.

Then late one moonless night, drawn by an inexplicable instinct, Farrah ventured out into the yawning darkness. She glided silently between the trees until a familiar rasping call sounded overhead.

"Ignitus!" she cried joyfully, spotting a glimmer of fiery plumage in the branches above.

The great phoenix spread his tattered wings and swooped down in front of her. "We meet again, child," he greeted warmly. "The night air refreshes your spirit?"

Farrah nodded. "It does. As does recalling your kind words." She hesitated shyly. "I was hoping we could talk more..."

"Of course. My purpose is to light the way for those traversing dark passages." Ignitus inclined his head, indicating for her to walk with him.

As they strolled beneath the stars, Farrah opened up about her ongoing struggles. The ancient phoenix listened intently, offering insights from his own journey to help bolster her when despair loomed.

By the time they returned to the edge of the woods, Farrah felt a renewed sense of hope. With Ignitus as her guide through the shadows, she could hold on until joy returned.

From then on, their nightly walks became a lifeline keeping Farrah afloat amidst the gloom. Each time she faltered, the phoenix was there, kindling her weakened spirit with his words. Together they would find the light again.

As the weeks went on, Farrah continued seeking solace in her nightly walks with Ignitus. His wise counsel helped her make sense of the hopelessness clouding her mind. Simply knowing someone understood was immensely comforting.

On darker nights when Farrah felt herself unravelling, the

phoenix would soothe her with reminders that the faint flickering of her inner fire was still enough to light the way forward. Even as the gale raged, he taught her to focus on each tentative step rather than the entirety of the tempest.

Other times, they walked in contemplative silence beneath the stars, the ancient phoenix radiating tranquil strength at her side. Farrah drew upon his timeless solidity like an anchor in her churning sea of despair.

When words failed, Ignitus would preen her dishevelled hair with his beak or sing soothing lullabies in his gravelly voice. His silent empathy conveyed what language could not. Under his protective wing, the young fairy felt less alone.

With Ignitus as her guardian through the darkest nights, Farrah nurtured the fragile seed of hope in her heart. Its tender shoots were easily battered, but with careful tending, she knew it would grow strong roots and blossom.

Each small sign of progress rekindled Farrah's flickering inner light - genuine laughter at the pixies' antics, admiring a perfect autumn leaf, managing to get out of bed on a leaden morning.

Like the wise phoenix reminding her, she needed only stay the course through harsh seasons, trusting the light would return. Sheltered and nurtured, her weakened spirit could heal.

One night, as Farrah and Ignitus walked through a silent glen blanketed in moonlight, the ancient phoenix turned to her with a thoughtful gleam in his golden eyes.

"Tell me, young one, what first kindled your spirit's fire?" he asked. "Before the winds turned harsh, what sights ignited your joy?"

Farrah considered the question. She thought back to her earliest memories - zipping carefree through the forest, playing tricks on her friends, spinning with arms outstretched beneath the sun.

"Laughter," she finally replied. "Bringing smiles and cheer to others lit me up from within."

Ignitus nodded sagely. "Then your path ahead is clear. If your gifts brought you joy, share them once more. Create beauty and light to guide others through darkness."

Farrah hesitated. "But I can barely muster the energy to care for myself now."

"Start small," advised Ignitus. "Plant seeds through little acts of kindness. In time, your gifts will bloom and multiply."

Inspired by the phoenix's wisdom, Farrah began focusing her hazy days on small gestures to lift friends' spirits. She left acorns on Edgar's doorstep, wove Willa flower crowns and whispered silly jokes to make the pixies giggle.

To her surprise, the sparks of joy her efforts kindled in others warmed her own depleted spirit too. Bit by bit, sharing her unique light with the world reignited Farrah's inner flame.

Each smile she coaxed out now fed Farrah's weary soul. With Ignitus' guidance, she was discovering how to nourish her gift despite winter's chill. Her laughter would echo through the forest once more.

One morning after a night's counsel with Ignitus, Farrah awoke feeling a sense of fiery determination flaring up within. Today would be different - she would actively push back against the fog's paralysis.

Farrah dressed in her favourite dress adorned with sunflowers carefully combed her golden hair and ate a full breakfast of berries and cream. Each small act of self-care kindled her inner glow a bit more.

Stepping outside, Farrah took a deep breath of the crisp autumn air. The breeze rippled through her wings, carrying the faint scent of woodsmoke and cinnamon. Somewhere nearby, friends were enjoying the seasonal festivities together.

Farrah set her shoulders. No more hiding away tending faint embers - it was time to embrace community and fun again. She took to the sky swiftly, letting muscle memory guide her to the pixie village.

The familiar laughter and singing grew louder as Farrah drew near. Suddenly, a tiny body zoomed toward her - Maya!

"Farrah!" the pixie exclaimed joyously. "You came!"

Other pixies and fairies gathered around, greeting her with

warm smiles and exclamations of delight. Their infectious excitement lit a blaze within Farrah. This was where she belonged.

Together they spent the golden day immersed in mischief and make-believe - weaving stealthy cloaks of leaves and grass to sneak up on friends, constructing tiny rafts to sail along the burbling creek and leaving each other playful scavenger hunts searching for fairy rings and other natural wonders nestled off the forest paths less travelled.

Seeing their ingenious hideouts and the unbridled creativity in details that Farrah had overlooked during her time in the fog filled her with awe. She resolved to always cherish the whimsy and magic of childhood; to never again take for granted how the simplest things could be made wondrous and new through imagination.

When at last the pixies had exhausted themselves with laughter and adventure, they begged Farrah for tales of her own childhood escapades now that she had rediscovered her spirit of daring imagination. They curled up eagerly at her feet as she regaled them with vivid stories - sneaking into the pixie bakery to filch honey cakes and leaving silly poems behind in payment, befriending a baby phoenix and helping him take his first flight, playing ingenious tricks on serious old Edgar that left him scratching his head in confusion much to their giggles.

As Farrah embellished each story with dramatic details, the pixies' eyes shone with delight, envisioning every narrow escape and magical encounter. They hung onto her every word with rapt wonder etched across their small faces. When the last story ended, they burst into ecstatic applause and pleas for more next time.

Farrah smiled contentedly, warmth flooding her heart. By immersing herself in their contagious joy and innocence again, she felt she had reconnected with that wide-eyed sense of play and lightness that the gloom had threatened to extinguish forever. Laughter came easily now, spilling out brightly again like bubbles dancing in the sunshine. Her inner flame was finally blazing fully once more.

Eventually, the pixies scampered off home for supper, still chattering excitedly about all of Farrah's stories and their grand adventures that day. Alone amidst the meadow wildflowers, Farrah sat reflecting as the sunset spilled stunning pink and gold across the horizon.

Later that night, resting cosily in bed, Farrah felt a swell of gratitude for having rejoined the dance of life once more. Kind words from loved ones echoed in her mind as she drifted off.

She felt fully at peace watching the dynamic colours slowly deepen and fade as dusk fell over the valley like a diaphanous veil. It seemed a metaphor for her own emergence from the darkness back into hope and light. By opening herself back up to laughter, friendship and beauty, she had bloomed once more.

As the last faint coral light disappeared fully into velvety night, a contented smile lingered on Farrah's lips. She made her way slowly home, wings pleasantly weary but heart overflowing with gratitude. The cold wind still nipped tentatively, but the coming days grew warmer and brighter each time the sun crested the distant hills. She could feel it now deep inside that her spirit had endured to blossom again.

Tomorrow the fog may creep in at the edges again. But tonight, she held the flickering candle Ignitus had helped nurture, protected from harsh winds. If she kept feeding its flame, someday it would blaze bold and bright again.

In the weeks that followed, Farrah continued to heed Ignitus' advice to nourish her spirit through community and kindness. Though she still struggled on gloomy days, she made an effort to push through the malaise.

On a morning when melancholy threatened to pin her in bed, Farrah forced herself to rise and visit the pixies. She sat quietly listening rather than engaging much, but little Maya's enthusiastic hug still warmed her heart.

Another day, Farrah collected acorns and autumn flowers to decorate her friends' homes. The creative process lifted her mood and seeing recipients' reactions to the gifts gave her a sense of purpose.

When the gloom felt too overwhelming for public outings, Farrah would work on art projects in private. She found painting and sewing soothing, losing herself in crafting until the darkness passed.

Ignitus reminded her often that surviving bleak days was enough - she needn't be lively or socialize if it taxed her stamina. "Rest and recovery enable you to blossom when the clouds part," he would say.

Farrah was slowly learning balance under the phoenix's guidance. Her inner fire remained fragile, but it burned on thanks to the love that sheltered it from harsh winds. She need only tend the embers until they blazed freely again.

On brighter days when laughter came easily, Farrah cherished feeling like her old self again. Holding onto those glimpses of joy gave her hope that the light would someday return for good.

With patient care, her flame would continue growing stronger. The long nights were slowly receding as dawn broke over the horizon at last.

As the weeks went on, Farrah felt herself gradually emerging from the gloom that had shrouded her spirit for so long. Under Ignitus' wise mentorship, she was learning strategies to kindle her inner light even through the darkest nights.

On mornings when melancholy still clung heavily, Farrah would will herself to rise and soak up the first rays of sunrise. Standing outside and breathing deeply helped clear the fog from her mind.

On other days, she found comfort in weaving dried flowers and grasses into wreaths to decorate her little cottage. The repetitive motions soothed her and seeing the fruits of her labour lifted her mood.

Cooking nourishing meals with ingredients from her garden also ignited motivation within Farrah. Following recipes focused her energy and filled her home with savoury aromas that stirred nostalgic happiness.

When loneliness crept in, Farrah would invite friends over to share in the bounty she created. Their laughter and gratitude for her gifts never failed to warm her spirit.

At night, Farrah recorded her progress and insights gained that day in a leather-bound journal. Writing helped process emotions she was still learning to articulate. Looking back on the past darkness gave her hope.

With Ignitus' infinite compassion lighting her way, Farrah was rediscovering her own gifts little by little. Each small step brought her closer to blooming fully once more. She needed only to nourish her spirit every day, trusting spring would come again.

One crisp night under the harvest moon, Ignitus led Farrah to a secluded hot spring nestled deep within the forest. As wisps of steam rose into the cold air, the phoenix let out a contented sigh.

"I thought you might find restorative powers in these healing waters, as I always have," he explained.

Farrah tentatively dipped a toe in and was instantly soothed by the warmth seeping into her skin. She sank gratefully into the spring, feeling weeks of tension dissolve.

Quiet fell over the glen, interrupted only by the gentle burbling of water over smooth stones. Farrah closed her eyes, overwhelmed with gratitude for Ignitus' wisdom in guiding her here tonight.

After a long meditative silence, the great phoenix spoke. "The path ahead will have tribulations still. But with care, your light will illuminate the way."

Farrah's eyes glistened with tears. "Words can't convey how much your friendship has meant to me through this darkness."

Ignitus placed a reassuring claw on her shoulder. "I am honoured to lend you my flames until yours burn true again. Have faith, young one."

That night, nestled in bed, Farrah journaled about Ignitus' unwavering support these long months. Even when she could not see her own strength, he had tended the embers of her spirit until they reignited once more. She hoped someday to pay such kindness forward.

For now, she would continue nourishing her own light with the phoenix's guidance. If she persisted through the darkest winters, spring's blossoming awaited. Hope was being reborn in her heart.

As the weeks went on, Farrah felt a sense of quiet confidence and inner peace slowly returning to her spirit. She was learning to be gentle with herself on darker days, while still doing small acts to kindle her depleted inner flame.

On weary mornings, she would sit by the creek writing in her journal or reading poetry rather than forcing false cheer. On other days when motivation flowed, she worked in her garden or visited the pixie village to spread light through laughter and song.

Farrah was careful not to overextend her fragile energy. With Ignitus' guidance, she prioritized rest and solitude when the fog crept close. The phoenix taught her that survival was courageous - thriving would come in time.

Slowly but surely, Farrah cultivated a routine that balanced gentle self-care with nurturing community connections. She found new wisdom in Ignitus' mantra to "plant seeds through little acts of love." Her gifts would blossom when the time was right.

With winter's chill taking hold, Farrah transformed her cottage into a cosy sanctum. She filled each room with fire-warmed stones, herbs, woven blankets and fresh pine boughs. On icy nights she cooked stew and invited friends to share in the warmth and comfort.

Though darker days inevitably came, she had built a shelter against the elements. Farrah had faith that she could weather any storm wrapped in the love surrounding her. Hope flickered brightly, guiding her forward.

As the first snow fell, blanketing the forest in shimmering white, Farrah felt a sense of tranquil peace settle upon her spirit. The land's quiet beauty reflected her inner stillness after months of turmoil.

On clear, cold nights when the stars burned brightly overhead, Farrah would meet Ignitus by the frozen creek. They sat in meditative silence as the phoenix radiated healing warmth to melt the icy shadows lingering in her heart.

One night, Ignitus unfurled his fiery wings to their full glory, casting dazzling reflections across the snow. "Your light too will rise unfettered again soon," he told Farrah. "Until then, let mine help guide your way."

Farrah's eyes shone with grateful tears. The phoenix's unwavering support had led her through the darkest valley back to hope. With him near, she could endure the coldest nights.

As the solstice neared, Ignitus encouraged Farrah to join in the village celebrations as she was able. She started by gifting loved ones simple homemade wreaths and baked goods. Seeing their joy rekindled her own creative spirit.

On the night of the solstice, Farrah ventured into the bustling village square. The sounds of music and laughter mingled with delicious aromas as fairies danced around a great bonfire.

Though she tired quickly, for the first time Farrah felt the warmth of community rather than isolation in her weariness. Surrounded by loved ones, she lifted her voice to the stars in joyful song once more.

As winter deepened, Farrah found comfort in simple rituals that connected her to friends and nature. On snowy mornings, she would sprinkle birdseed and lay out fresh water for the forest animals. Watching them flock to her garden lifted her spirits.

Baking bread and winding woollen scarves for her fellow fairies also ignited Farrah's creativity within the winter stillness. Kneading fragrant dough and stitching colourful yarn were meditative rituals that eased her lingering melancholy.

When loneliness crept in, Farrah would invite Willa over to cook hearty potato stew together. They would sit by the fire afterwards sipping rosehip tea and chatting long into the cold nights. Their easy rapport warmed Farrah to her core.

On clearer days when she felt strong enough, Farrah visited the pixies to sculpt whimsical snow fairies and have snowball fights. Their mirthful laughter stirred long-absent dimples in her cheeks.

At night, Farrah continued writing by firelight in her leather-bound journal. She wrote of hope rekindled and skills rediscovered, of friendships deepened through adversity. Each page honoured the light she found even in the darkest season.

And when the ice beckoned her into the gloom, Ignitus still

stood sentinel, thawing her heart with ancient wisdom. "Every storm runs its course," he would remind her. "This too shall pass."

Sheltered and sustained through winter's fury, the seeds Farrah had planted would blossom anew. Spring was on its way.

As the days slowly lengthened again, Farrah began to feel the stirrings of renewal within her spirit. While she still had some gloomy days, hope burned brighter now like the first pale green buds pushing up through snow.

On clearer mornings, Farrah would rise with the sun and walk through the forest, watching icicles glitter and melt as dawn's light streamed through the canopy. The sound of dripping water was a balm to her weary soul.

The fresh earthy scents of newly exposed soil and sprouting roots invigorated Farrah's senses. She would linger over small wonders - fuzzy pussy willows, tiny red chickadee songs, the rush of sap in thawing birch trees. Each sign of nature awakening reawakened her own tired spirit.

Ignitus observed Farrah's growing strength with deep pride. "You see?" he would say. "The longest nights herald brightest dawns."

Farrah smiled up at the phoenix, eyes shining. "You stayed by my side through the darkness. Now let us walk into springtime together."

Ignitus wrapped her in his wing's comforting warmth. After the isolating winter, Farrah was ready to fully blossom again. With loved ones around her, she boldly stepped forward to embrace spring's rebirth.

The quickening energy of the earth was contagious. Farrah felt creativity and joy kindling her from within once more. Soon she would be ablaze again, her gifts shining brightly for all to see.

As the last frosts relinquished their grip on the land, Farrah felt her spirit thawing and unfurling like the tender new leaves around her. After the isolating winter, she was ready to fully blossom again.

On sunny afternoons, Farrah visited the pixie village, where makeshift markets bustled with activity. She took in the sights and smells of fresh flowers, ripe produce, herbs and baked goods that reminded her of simpler times.

Wandering slowly from stall to stall, Farrah felt herself relaxing into the cheerful din of commerce and community. Pausing to listen to a street musician or sample a sweet honey tart brought her childlike joy.

With encouragement from Ignitus, Farrah began sharing her own talents again too. She set up a booth selling intricate wreaths, soaps and dried flower arrangements. Though she often tired quickly, the delight her creations sparked kindled her inner flame.

At home, Farrah spent long afternoons gardening, breathing life back into the earth alongside her own spirit. Tending soil, planting seeds, watching new growth unfurl - each brought profound peace after winter's desolation.

In the boundless optimism of spring, Farrah felt hope flourishing within once more. Her gifts had endured the bitter cold. Now she could begin blossoming fully again, renewed appreciation for life's beauty kindled in her heart.

As spring's renewal took hold across the land, Farrah felt a joyful energy returning to her spirit. After winter's stillness, she was ready to dance again.

On sunny days, Farrah would soar across vibrant meadows, looping and diving through the sweet air. Feeling the wind in her hair and the sun on her wings ignited her from within.

The hypnotic buzzing of bees and chirping of birdsong echoed Farrah's delighted laughter. Seeing new life abounding throughout nature mirrored her inner transformation.

In the evenings, Farrah would meet with friends in the forest Glen that had gone abandoned during the cold months. Now fireflies flickered in the air as they shared food and music together once more.

Making wreaths of luminous flowers, Farrah and the pixies danced and played games till night fell. Then they lay gazing up at the stars, feeling small but connected to the vast cosmos.

With Ignitus' ever-watchful and patient presence nearby, Farrah opened her spirit to spring's magic. She let go of lingering gloom, embracing rebirth. After such an isolating winter, it felt incredible to play and sing freely under the sun again.

The phoenix nodded approvingly, seeing Farrah blossom. "Your light was only dormant for a season," he told her. "Now it is rekindled ever brighter."

One cool spring night, Farrah flew to the tranquil hot springs where Ignitus had first brought her months ago. How far she had come since that bleak evening of despair. Now Farrah's heart overflowed with gratitude.

As if summoned by her thoughts, the great phoenix emerged from the moonlit mist. Ignitus' eyes shone with deep pride for his student and her profound resilience.

Farrah rushed forward to embrace him. "Your wisdom guided me through the darkest winter," she said. "Now here we stand in spring, our hopes reborn."

Ignitus enveloped her in his crimson wings. "I merely fanned the embers until your inner fire blazed once more. You always carried that light within."

Farrah knew the phoenix spoke the truth. Even when she had lost sight of the stars, their light had endured through the night. She had survived to see the dawn.

"I will stay the course you set me on," Farrah promised. "And help others find their way through darkness too."

Ignitus smiled gently. "Then my purpose here is fulfilled. Your gifts are needed now, little one. Let your bold spirit take flight once more."

Farrah watched tearfully as the wise phoenix dissolved into flickering embers that drifted up to join the constellations. His light would guide her forever.

Turning her face skyward, Farrah closed her eyes and embraced the peace of this moment. She was ready to fly forward, spirit renewed. Her inner flame burned bright again at last.

Chapter 4: Taking Flight

A few weeks had passed since Ignitus, the wise old phoenix, had helped rekindle hope in Farrah's weary spirit. Though he was gone, his gentle guidance remained imprinted on her heart, urging her forward even through the gloomiest days.

On this morning, Farrah awoke feeling the familiar weight pressing down on her, trying to pin her wings and spirit back into the darkness she had only recently emerged from. The sunlight streaming through her window only seemed to accentuate the leaden darkness clouding her mind.

She wanted nothing more than to pull the covers over her head and sink back into oblivion. But Ignitus' voice echoed in her thoughts, reminding her to focus on progress in small steps.

With a resigned sigh, Farrah forced her leaden body upright and dragged herself out of bed. The simple act of dressing felt oddly exhausting, as though she were trying to fly through dense fog. She stared numbly at her reflection in the looking glass as she worked a comb through her rumpled golden locks. The fairy staring back looked utterly depleted, eyes dim and shoulders slumped in defeat

Farrah's gaze fell on the dried wildflowers she had picked with such joy only yesterday, now wilting in their vase. They reminded her of the heaviness seeping back into her bones, muting her inner light once more. She turned away in frustration, overcome by the sheer unfairness of it. Hadn't she just regained her spirit? Why did the darkness still cling so?

Shuffling to her kitchen, Farrah prepared a plain breakfast of oatmeal, chewing each flavourless bite of the bland food mechanically. After washing up, she stood at her doorway, staring at the impossibly bright and cheerful world outside.

The very thought of venturing out into the bustling village square made her stomach clench anxiously. Farrah was tempted to retreat back to bed. But she imagined Ignitus' gently prodding voice, encouraging her not to isolate herself.

"Right...just a quick walk to get some fresh air," Farrah muttered to herself. Taking a deep breath, she stepped outside into the sunlight which immediately stung her sensitive eyes.

Keep moving, she told herself, trying not to succumb to the impulse to turn tail and flee home. She kept her gaze fixed on the path ahead, avoiding eye contact with the cheerful fairies flitting about. Each step was a struggle, but Farrah kept her eyes fixed straight ahead as she made her way along the pathway. Simply navigating the cacophony of sights and sounds felt jarringly overwhelming for Farrah's senses that morning

After a few agonizing minutes of dodging social interaction, Farrah found herself in a quieter part of the woods. Her breathing eased slightly once out of the crowded village centre. This was enough progress for today.

As she turned toward home, Farrah spied a patch of vibrant wildflowers growing along the path. Their bright petals were the only colour cutting through the dull grey fog in her mind.

Inspired, she knelt down and began slowly gathering up purple asters, goldenrods and other lush blossoms, letting the simple task soothe her racing thoughts. Farrah closed her eyes as she ran her fingers over the delicate petals, taking comfort in their velvety texture and sweet herbal scent. The rest of the world fell away for a moment.

Clutching her bouquet, she turned towards home where she was finally able to release a shaky sigh. The morning had thoroughly depleted what meagre energy she had woken up with.

As she placed the wildflowers in a vase by her window, Farrah was surprised to feel a faint sense of accomplishment after such a difficult morning. It was a small victory, but sustaining her fragile equilibrium took daily courage. She would persist, little by little.

That night, Farrah wrote in her journal by candlelight of her struggles that day, but also the tiny triumph of the flowers, proof she still had light within her worth kindling. She knew from experience now this darkness would pass again if she continued wading through the inky fog until she, at last, emerged into dawn. With rest and care, she would make it there again. Until then, endurance was its own quiet resilience.

In the weeks that followed, Farrah continued taking small but meaningful steps forward with the memory of Ignitus' wisdom guiding her. Though the path was daunting, focusing on incremental progress gave her hope.

On darker mornings, when her limbs felt made of stone. Farrah made an effort to rise with the sun's first light rather than succumbing to melancholy in bed. Standing outside breathing the dawn air helped clear the fog from her mind, knowing that being surrounded by nature's beauty often lifted her mood slightly. She focused on details of sensory wonder - the satisfying crunch of leaves underfoot, cold creek water refreshing her bare feet and the spicy scent of wildflowers tickling her nose.

When melancholia overwhelmed her, Farrah tried to honour it mindfully rather than spiralling into shame and self-blame as she once had. She became an observer of her emotions, journaling about their ebbs and flows. Giving them space to just be without judgment allowed her spirit to rest.

Farrah also discovered that spending time cooking or baking, especially to gift loved ones, centred her fraying mind in the present moment. Kneading fragrant dough, chopping colourful vegetables, infusing sugar with flower essences - the humble rituals of crafting nourishment made her feel capable again even on hollow days.

When loneliness crept in, she made an effort to visit Edgar or Willa for tea and easy conversation. Farrah focused on riding out the discomfort she felt engaged socially until the tension released its grip. Their quiet company and compassion lifted her spirits without taxing her limited energy reserves. She was deeply grateful for their stalwart loyalty through every wax and wane.

Farrah also discovered that spending time cooking or baking, especially to gift loved ones, became another comforting ritual for Farrah. Kneading the dough soothed her nerves and seeing recipients' delight warmed her heart. The humble rituals of crafting nourishment made her feel capable again even on hollow days.

On lighter days when motivation bubbled up, Farrah tried to seize on it by doing activities that sparked creativity or purpose within - pressing leaves and flowers, making floral wreaths and venturing farther into the vibrant autumn forests alone to forage for pine cones and seed pods.

Accomplishing these small acts of beauty or service ignited a glimmer of warmth and meaning inside her once more. Farrah was gently rediscovering how to spread light again even from the shadows where she so often dwelt. Progress was not linear or constant, but it was progress nonetheless. She clung to that knowledge during the valleys between each hard-won peak.

There were still setbacks where depression darkened her door once more. But Farrah was learning not to criticize herself during those times. As Ignitus had taught her, surviving bleak periods took courage in itself.

By following the phoenix's advice to take small steps forward when possible, pause when needed and ask for support, Farrah found the light growing gradually brighter. Recovery was a marathon, not a sprint - but she was finding her stride again.

As the weeks went on, Farrah felt her energy and motivation continuing to grow through maintaining the small self-care habits Ignitus had encouraged. There were inevitable setbacks, but she pushed through them with courage. She was learning not to judge herself harshly in either season.

On weary mornings, Farrah still made an effort to rise with the sun. Standing outside breathing deeply helped clear away the cobwebs of gloom still clinging to her mind.

On darker mornings, Farrah practised granting herself grace - sleeping in when needed, meditating by her window with chamomile tea, writing affirmations in her journal reminding her inner light still shone behind the clouds. Simply being kind to herself through the gloom took great courage.

On other days when creativity trickled back, rejuvenating her spirit, Farrah tried to embrace it fully. She would bake berry tarts or spiced nut breads to deliver warm from the oven to loved ones. Letting her gifts flow freely left her feeling uplifted and purposeful again.

When she craved solitude, Farrah allowed herself quiet time wandering through crimson autumn forests alone to absorb the beauty and introspect. But she also pushed past her comfort zone to attend community meals or play gentle games with the pixies, not letting fear of fatigue halt her progress.

When she felt more sociable, Farrah visited the pixies' village to chat or play gentle games in the meadow for short intervals before retreating home to recharge. She forced herself to giggle and play along and found their infectious joy slowly rubbed off on her too although she was careful to set boundaries and honour her limits.

Through it all, she listened closely to her evolving needs, sometimes indulging melancholy mindfully when it called, other times gently nudging herself back into the light once more. Farrah knew from experience now she possessed the inner resilience to endure these ups and downs while moving ever forward.

At night, she recorded her thoughts on the day's particular challenges and triumphs, insights gained and hopes kindled. Journaling became an important practice for processing emotions. Holding space to honour every emotional season without judgment fostered equilibrium even amidst the storms. And writing reminded her she had survived the darkness before - she would emerge stronger again.

There were still darker days when getting out of bed felt like trying to fly through quicksand. But Farrah gave herself permission to rest, remembering progress was not linear. Simply maintaining equilibrium through the setbacks kept her moving forward.

Like Ignitus taught her, thriving takes time after the spirit has been battered by storms. But each small step brought Farrah closer to rediscovering inner stability and wings strong enough for joyful flight.

As autumn shifted into winter's chill, Farrah felt the familiar

CHAPTER 4: TAKING FLIGHT

gloom beckoning, eager to dim her spirit's glow once more. But this year, she drew strength from the knowledge that she had persevered through harsh seasons before. She would withstand again.

Each frosty morning, Farrah forced herself to rise before the sunrise. She would stand vigil as the darkness gradually ceded to the thin light with growing patience and reverence, solemnly welcoming the dawn. Ritual fostered meaning.

Keeping her hands occupied also helped quiet racing thoughts on more anxious days. Farrah turned to creative projects - lavender wreaths for the solstice, embroidered quilts, whittling trinket boxes from pine to hold secret treasures. The mindful process soothed her nerves and centred her in purpose.

When melancholy crept too close for comfort, Farrah would invite Willa over for long fireside chats over mugs of cinnamon tea. Or she would bundle up and venture out to Edgar's cottage, where laughter and music with friends lessened isolation's vice grip. Their presence through the difficult moments fortified her immensely.

At night, Farrah recorded all she still had to be grateful for, despite the looming darkness - the ethereal beauty of new snow under the moonlight, a perfectly ripe persimmon's sweetness, the cosiness of woollen blankets, unconditional love from friends. The light remained everywhere, if she but opened her eyes to it, ready to kindle her spirit again.

The winter fog still obscured at times, but Farrah now weathered it with hard-earned wisdom. She drew strength from Ignitus' deep, gentle voice echoing in her mind - "You are stronger than this, child. Keep your inner fire lit." With compassion and community, she would stay the course once more. Spring approached.

As winter deepened, Farrah found comfort in small daily rituals that brought light and meaning to the monotonous, melancholy days. Though the darkness still came in bleak waves, she had tools now to nurture her depleted spirit until the cold relinquished its harsh grip.

Each pale morning, Farrah would arise early to watch the nascent sunrise gild the frozen landscape in gold, breathing purposefully to centre her mind and open it to the coming day's possibility. Then she moved with reverence through quiet rituals - lighting fragrant candles, baking wholesome bread, speaking affirmations into the ether.

On especially gloomy days, Farrah forced herself outdoors even for just brief moments, knowing isolating indoors could exacerbate despair. She focused on the stark beauty surrounding her - the way snow muffled a songbird's melody, bare birches etched delicately against grey skies, smoke ribboning from a neighbour's chimney. Stillness fostered insight.

When she yearned for connection and levity, Farrah would stop by Willa or Edgar's cottage to share freshly baked currant scones straight from her oven. Their easy laughter and rapport never failed to lift her weary spirit. She drew strength too from their awe at her resilience through yet another harsh winter.

Before retiring each night, Farrah wrote sincerely in her journal about all she still had to be grateful for, though freshly grieved over each time - the subtle solar shifts marking time's steady progress, healing scents of cinnamon and cedar filling her home, dear friends who never wavered through the seasons. Hope waited patiently to be unearthed and tended. She had only to nurture its fragile seeds as she had learned, trusting in time's slow but sacred rhythms. Spring would bloom in time.

As the solstice approached marking the turning point of the year, Farrah felt a familiar melancholy threaten to consume the inner light she had so painstakingly kindled. But this year, she clung to the approaching dawn. The darkest hour came right before daybreak and illuminated all shadow.

On the longest nights, she lay wakeful, Farrah focused on the incremental solar shifts she had observed, reminding herself the darkness' reign was not infinite. She found catharsis too in channelling brewing emotions into poetry and stark charcoal drawings by firelight, purging pain into creation.

Though she remained mostly secluded during this peak period of gloom, Farrah made an effort to partake in solstice ceremonies with trusted loved ones who understood her struggles. Simple rituals such as adorning a pine bough with runes for hope while circling a bonfire filled her spirit with much-needed levity and awe at enduring mythos.

The nights felt endless, but Farrah clung to promise in metaphor - yule logs burning down to reveal hidden gold inside, the sun's invisible journey creeping slowly but indefatigably northward again. She had survived this abyss before. Each small act of devotion brought spring nearer. Her flickering light just needed patience and shelter from harsh winds until it could shine freely once more.

Soon the ice would thaw, the darkness lift and her soul would be bathed in radiance again. Until then, Farrah tended her fragile inner flame diligently through the last bitter nights of winter's fury. This too would pass; dawn would break again. She needed only to hold fast.

As winter's harshness gradually gave way and spring's renewal took hold across the land, Farrah felt her own spirit lifting in tandem. The sun's warmth on her face and vivid new growth filling the forest mirrored the hope kindling inside her after a long, cold winter.

Each morning she awoke in time to witness the nascent sunrise, paying devout attention to the thin shards of light slowly illuminating the inky woods outside her frosted window. She honoured these incremental shifts out of the darkness that mirrored the thawing of winter's grip on her own heavy heart.

On brighter days when energy flowed, Farrah visited the bustling pixie village market. She took in the music, laughter and tempting scents of baked goods that reminded her of simpler times. Pausing to listen to a street musician or sample a honey tart brought childlike joy.

Other times, she meandered slowly through the woods gathering herbs, mushrooms and wildflowers. Farrah would use her bounty to craft salves, teas and balms in her cosy cottage, finding comfort in the ritual. Concocting remedies made her feel capable again.

When exhaustion crept in, she gave herself permission to spend quiet days at home to practice self-care rituals like curling up with books of poetry and sipping chamomile tea. Farrah was learning to honour her emotional limits without shame or judgment. Surviving the valleys between peaks of joy again took profound courage.

Farrah spent many days with beloved friends tidying cottages, raking lawns and preparing their gardens together for spring planting in anticipation of future bounty. Turning over the thawed soil with bare hands reminded them all of the dormancy's purpose - dark seasons strengthened roots.

Before retiring each night, she recorded her thoughts in her leather-bound journal by candlelight. Under Ignitus' guidance, she had survived the darkest winter. Now Farrah felt ready to fully blossom again, reborn with the land.

On weary days, she remembered the phoenix's mantra - "Healing takes time, progress comes slowly." She would grow strong again soon. For now, each step forward was a triumph.

As warmer days arrived, Farrah began venturing farther from her cottage into the forest paths and meadows she had long missed. The sweet aromas of wildflowers and the sound of babbling streams called to her spirit.

At first, the walks left her easily fatigued, both physically and emotionally. But Farrah knew that persevering little by little would rebuild her endurance. She often paused to rest or turn back when it became too much.

With time and consistency, the hikes grew easier. Farrah found herself able to go further while still pacing herself gently. Exploring old haunts ignited nostalgia and renewed appreciation for the beauty surrounding her.

When she felt up to more activity, Farrah would join the young pixies playing tag and other games that stretched her movement in joyful ways. Their laughter brought out her own.

On cooler days when melancholy lingered, Farrah was learning not to chide herself. Instead, she would work on crafts at home, write in her journal and reread Ignitus' wise words until her spirit realigned.

It was a gradual uphill climb. But focusing on how far she had come rather than how far there was to go kept Farrah's wings uplifted. With resilient hope kindled in her heart, she felt ready to truly take flight again soon.

Over the next few weeks, Farrah focused on integrating the little coping strategies the phoenix had taught her. She pushed herself to get outside and move most days, even just brief strolls around the meadow.

When energy trickled back, Farrah accompanied the young pixies on rambling wanders through the forest to admire spring's early glories - fuzzy pussy willows, green shoots poking up through decaying leaves, Ravens cawing hoarsely as they circled overhead through shafts of sunlight. Each detail of awakening filled her with joy.

The quickening energy was infectious. Soon Farrah happily joined in play again - floating leaf boats along the creek, playing hide and seek amidst the lacy lichen and moss-blanketed tree trunks. Laughter left her flushed and full of life once more. She felt a childlike wonder rekindled within her spirit.

Some days the fog still felt all-consuming, making even small tasks require monumental effort. On those grey mornings, Farrah gave herself permission to rest and simply survive. Just maintaining her progress through the setbacks mattered.

With Ignitus' wise voice in her heart reminding her to be gentle, Farrah found the turbulence slowly smoothing. She was learning to bank the inner fire needed to keep momentum through the darkest seasons. Bit by bit, day by day, she would take flight again.

One breezy sunny morning, Farrah awoke feeling a sense of fiery determination, she threw open her shutters and breathed in the sweet floral air. Today felt different - there was change rippling through her spirit. Today would be the day she tried flying at full speed again. Starting slowly over the past weeks had helped prepare her wings for this milestone. The time had come to fully spread her wings again

She dressed swiftly, donning a shimmery dress that matched

the renewed sparkle in her eyes. She twirled around her room, unable to contain the energy flowing through her.

After eating a hearty breakfast, Farrah took a deep breath and strode out into the golden morning light. The birdsong and flower scents greeted her vibrant senses. She stood tall, closed her eyes and unfurled her crystalline wings to their full span. Then, with bold grace, she began flapping them faster and faster until her feet lifted off the ground.

With a joyful laugh, she took off swift and straight as an arrow released from its bow. The wind whipped against Farrah's smiling face as she rocketed through the crisp air. It had been so long!

Higher and higher Farrah climbed, her eyes drinking in the stunning vista around her - emerald forest awaking, wildflowers waving, rolling hills beyond. With the wind rushing against her smiling face, she let out an exhilarated laugh.

Farrah swooped and danced through the crisp air, loops growing wider, dives more daring. She had forgotten this feeling - the boundless freedom of flight, the tranquillity of floating upon the wind. She performed looping somersaults, heart soaring at the freedom of motion. Farrah revelled in reuniting with the sky, her natural element and sanctuary. This must be how baby birds felt on their first flights.

As Farrah soared over the forest, pixies and fairies paused their bustling to gaze up in awe. "Look, it's Farrah!" they cried joyfully. "She has come back to us!" They cheered her on, faces beaming.

Farrah alighted gently amidst her friends, eyes glistening with joyful tears. She had made it through the darkest winter back to spring. Now her spirit shone brighter than ever, wings stronger from the tempest they had weathered.

Waving down at the cheering pixies, Farrah shot straight up and broke through the forest canopy. She paused, hovering and breathless, to admire the verdant sea of treetops spreading below.

As she gently floated down, Farrah felt overwhelming gratitude for the simple gifts of flight, nature and body in sync. Today, she had reclaimed the unfettered joy that was her birthright. Ignitus would be so proud.

That night, she wrote happily in her journal: 'Today I flew as fast as I dared and found myself again. The only direction left is forward.'

With hope and care, she had kindled her inner flame once more. Now Farrah was truly ready to fly forward into the light.

Buoyed by reclaiming the freedom of flight, Farrah awoke the next morning feeling ready to continue expanding her world. She decided to visit a favourite childhood spot - a secluded meadow filled with wildflowers and butterflies.

The journey left her pleasantly tired but not drained. As Farrah crested the hill overlooking the meadow, she paused, overcome by nostalgia. How she had loved frolicking here as a child without a care!

Farrah spent the afternoon chasing butterflies amidst the swaying blooms. Seeing familiar birds and rabbits still flocking to the meadow filled her with comfort. This safe space welcomed her back.

On the walk home, Farrah reflected on how flying and exploring alone used to energize her. While she still cherished solitude, opening herself back up to community had rekindled a missing brightness in her spirit.

Arriving home, Farrah was greeted by the enthusiastic shouts and waves of young pixies. "Welcome back!" they chorused. Once their commotion would have overwhelmed her, but now it simply warmed her heart.

That night, Farrah wrote in her journal about the restorative gifts of nature and friendship. With help, she was rediscovering how to savour life's simple joys again. She felt closer to her true self than she had in a long time.

There were still challenges ahead, but Ignitus had set her soaring. Each flight made her wings stronger. With perseverance and support, the clouds in her mind would continue to dissipate, revealing an open sky ahead.

In the weeks that followed, Farrah felt herself truly taking flight again after being grounded for so long. She continued expanding her world little by little, reconnecting with people and activities that ignited her diminished spirit.

On days when she had more energy, Farrah began helping out around the village - running errands for elderly neighbours, lending a hand at the bakery, delivering surplus garden produce to families in need. Keeping busy lifted her mood and she enjoyed being useful again.

Back home, Farrah spent hours studying herb seed catalogues and sketching garden plans. She neatly sorted and cleaned the tools shed that had gathered dust during her depressive episodes until they gleamed. The promise of planting and nurturing new life stirred her creative spirit after its long hibernation.

At twilight, she led friends on leisurely wanders to notice rebirth's wonders - songbirds proclaiming territories, green buds embroidering the barren branches that had awed her with their resilience, the creek's rush gaining power and purpose again. Bearing witness together awakened hope.

Farrah looked forward with brightening eyes to blooming fully along with the land. Gentle rains had replenished her thirsty spirit; the light had called her out of the darkness once more. Now she turned her face up boldly to embrace spring's long-awaited return. Ready to unfold again, she danced forth lightly to greet the sunny days ahead.

No matter how she spent her days, Farrah made sure to leave time for reflection. She wrote in her journal nightly, took walks alone in the woods and retreated to her cottage when she was weary. Ignitus had taught her that listening inwardly was as important as engaging outwardly.

By honouring her evolving needs each day, Farrah found equilibrium and joy. She was like a young bird strengthening her wings little by little before surging high into the sky. Soon she would soar freely once more.

As the weeks went on, Farrah felt herself truly soaring again for the first time since the darkness had clouded her spirit. She delighted in looping through crisp autumn skies and letting the wind dance through her golden hair.

Willa, Edgar and all her friends remarked on the renewed radiance shining from within Farrah. They had missed her levity and enthusiastic spirit. Now seeing her thrive again filled them with joy.

At night, curled up with Spot, Farrah felt profound gratitude for the support that had lifted her through the darkest clouds. She had emerged wiser, with deeper reserves of resilience to draw from.

Farrah knew that she would likely face future challenges and intervals of sadness. But Ignitus had helped kindle an inner light that could withstand even the fiercest storms. She was ready to move forward, spirit renewed.

One crisp spring morning, Farrah awoke feeling a surge of energy and purpose. Today she would gather her dearest friends and lead them on an adventure, just like old times.

She zoomed around inviting everyone to meet at the meadow overlooking the valley. Willa and Edgar arrived and then Maya showed up with a gaggle of young pixies. Seeing Farrah so vibrant again brought them infectious joy.

"Come, my friends, the forest awaits!" Farrah cried enthusiastically, before diving off the cliff's edge and soaring swiftly as an arrow towards the trees below. The others whooped and cheered, following her lead.

Farrah led them on a trek through the woods, forging paths, climbing trees and crossing stepping-stone rivers. The pixies scampered to match her pace, thrilled to see her relishing life again.

Pausing by a burbling stream, they shared the snacks they had packed while Farrah pointed out unique plants and animals. She had always had a gift for discovering wonder in nature's details.

As the sun sank low, they lay looking up at the darkening sky scattered with the first twinkling stars. Farrah's heart swelled at the beauty and simplicity of this perfect day with loved ones.

Later at home, she wrote passionately in her journal of the unfettered joy exploration had awakened within her. For the first time in forever, she felt truly free and alive again.

Farrah awoke the next morning still buzzing with inspiration from the previous day's adventure. She decided to spend today cultivating her long-neglected creative gifts.

After breakfast, she gathered art supplies - paints, brushes, coloured pencils, embroidery floss - and set up facing the open window. A breeze rippled through chimes as the morning light streamed in.

Farrah's paintbrush flowed gracefully as she brought vivid forest scenes to life - shimmering rivers, sunlight dappling through leaves, a majestic phoenix soaring over treetops. Losing herself in colour and motion felt hypnotic.

Later, she began stitching a landscape embroidery hoop with silken threads in emerald, sunflower and sapphire. Weaving the scene stitched her spirit back together too in a way. Each pull of the needle was an act of healing.

When her eyes grew weary, Farrah stepped outside into the soft twilight. Scattering seeds for the birds centred her mind. She stood reflecting as their melodic songs filled the darkening sky.

That night, Farrah wrote of the catharsis creativity had reawakened within her. She had rediscovered so many lost parts of herself on this journey. Now she was ready to fully shine her unique light again.

The road ahead still stretched far. But with wings tested by storms and a heart full of gratitude, she was prepared to continue her flight upward.

In the weeks that followed, Farrah felt her creativity flourishing again as she poured energy into projects that brought purpose and peace. Though she still had some low days, immersing herself in artwork often lifted her spirit.

In the late evening sitting outside under the stars, Farrah knew she still had inner wounds to tend. But she had been given precious gifts - wisdom, resilience and an unquenchable inner flame to rely on during future storms. With hope and patience, she would continue to grow stronger.

Chapter 5: Parting the Clouds

As the verdant summer days shifted gently into autumn's vibrant hues, Farrah often found herself reflecting with gratitude on the light she had painstakingly rekindled within after such a long and desolate night. Though inevitable shadows still came, her inner glow now burned too bright to be extinguished again.

Farrah glided slowly through the forest undergrowth, pausing to touch the leaves that were morphing from green to rich shades of amber and garnet. She made a point to pause and truly notice splendour often overlooked - spiderwebs glittering like lace, sunlight dappling the undergrowth, squirrels chattering secrets to one another from their leafy perches overhead.

She let awe wash over her again and again. Autumn was in full swing now. She smiled as a chestnut dropped from an overhead branch right into her outstretched palm.

Reflecting on the changing seasons, Farrah felt a swell of gratitude in her heart. She had weathered spring's rebirth and summer's warmth after enduring such a long and isolating winter. With the unwavering support of loved ones, she had kindled her inner light once more.

Yet Farrah knew that maintaining her equilibrium would require continued vigilance and care. On weary days, melancholy still crept in like gnarled fingers grasping at her wings. Recovery was a lifelong journey, not a final destination.

But Farrah tried not to let those darker moments discourage

her progress. She focused on all she had regained - creativity, community and a spirit fortified by adversity. Emerging from the valley had reshaped her forever.

As Farrah made her way through the woods back home, she spotted Edgar up ahead waving cheerily. Though socializing still drained her some days, she no longer avoided friends for fear of burdening them. Their care had carried her through the storms.

"Hello, Edgar!" Farrah called, mustering a smile. "It's a lovely crisp day, perfect for the harvest."

"It is indeed!" the elf replied. "Plenty of mushrooms after those autumn rains. How about you join me gathering?"

Farrah's first instinct was to decline and retreat home. But the subtle uplift in Edgar's expression made her reconsider. Bringing him joy kindled light within her too.

"I'd love that," she accepted warmly. Together they continued down the forest path, chatting lightly about the changing colours and foraging bounty. Farrah let the beauty around her lift her spirit.

Later that night, curled up in her cosy cottage, Farrah reflected on how saying yes to small moments of connection continued fuelling her growth, even on heavier days. Darkness still wandered at the wood's edge, but love kept it at bay.

In the weeks that followed, Farrah continued taking life one day at a time, focusing on finding small sources of peace or purpose to see her through both upbeat days and melancholy ones.

On gloomier days still when steel-wool clouds obscured the sun and rain pattered softly but insistently against her cottage windows, Farrah reached without hesitation now for the comforting rituals that had become her routines of gentle self-care over the changing seasons—curling up in her favourite patched quilt with a steaming mug of rosehip tea to write poetry or prose in her leather-bound journal, or simply sitting by the fire to watch the leaves swirling down from the silvery sky outside.

She showed herself compassion without judgment on these darker days, lovingly allowing any turbulent emotions to simply run their course until they passed naturally on their own. Farrah no longer struggled against the tides of melancholy when they came washing in but rather sank into them as she would a warm bath, trusting they would soon recede again leaving her cleansed.

Whenever the cold gloom still threatened to creep in and drag her spirit back down into those familiar, foggy valleys of despair again, Farrah swiftly turned towards the light— stepping outside to soak up a sunbeam breaking suddenly through the clouds, taking deep breaths among the earthy scent of the woods after a rain, reminding herself that just as day must always follow night, so too would this shadow pass in time.

She drew strength always from looking back and remembering all she had slowly overcome and survived thus far, step by shaky step. Farrah knew now in her soul that the warm light still flickered steadily within her heart, ready to be gently coaxed into radiance again through the gentle kindling of self-love and care. With this knowledge, she was able to learn to stand tall once more, boldly looking forward instead of back.

At summer's bittersweet end marked by roaring bonfires under starlit skies, Farrah's voice joined the others in joyful song and laughter once more, the reflection of flames ablaze in her eyes. She was reminded of her spirit—injured and tested ruthlessly by the extended fury of past winters, but eventually emerging renewed, a phoenix rising from the ashes to burn all the brighter now. With this deepened wisdom and resilience ignited within, she was ready to turn bravely to whatever lay on the road ahead, unafraid.

When creativity flowed, she would paint vibrant forest scenes or bake savoury vegetable potpies to share with Willa and Edgar. Immersing herself in crafting uplifted her spirit and spreading that joy to others multiplied it.

Farrah also made an effort to say yes to friends' invitations when possible, rather than isolate herself due to fear or fatigue. Even just brief visits for tea could brighten her day and strengthen her resilience.

There were still setbacks where the light dimmed. But Farrah was learning not to judge herself. With rest and care, her inner glow would return. She focused on maintaining equilibrium through ups and downs.

At night, Farrah reflected in her journal on all she had overcome already. With patience and support, she knew the darkness could be held at bay once more. Her spirit would continue brightening, little by little each day.

As the weeks went on, Farrah had good days where her energy and enthusiasm felt boundless and she delighted in playing tricks and bringing laughter to the village once more. But melancholy still visited from time to time, dimming her spirit.

As the days grew shorter and the nights became gradually more crisp, Farrah felt a profound sense of tranquillity settle over her spirit. She had always loved the autumn season, but now its poignant beauty held deeper layers of meaning after the valleys she had walked through.

Each morning she would arise with the sun's first slant-ing amber rays and wander slowly through forests trans-formed overnight into vivid palettes of ruby, garnet and gold. The rustling melody of leaves swirling down from overhead branches filled her ears as she paused often to appraise nature's fleeting masterpieces - maples crowned in flame, heavy persimmons dangling like gilded ornaments, networks of delicate bejewelled spiderwebs.

When rain fell instead, drumming rhythmically upon her cottage roof, Farrah would settle herself by the windowsill with a cracked leather tome of poetry in her lap. She savoured the earthy petrichor scents wafting in on the damp breeze as she paused thoughtfully between poems about the quickening march of time towards winter. Rain nurtured introspection.

On other days, summoning her strength, Farrah would still force herself to visit the pixies or participate in community activities. Even just managing a brief social interaction before retreating home felt like an accomplishment on darker days.

When she craved the comforting warmth of community, Farrah brought deliveries of freshly pressed cider and homemade apple tarts still piping hot to the doorsteps of dear loved ones. Seeing their pleased surprise upon receiving her small offerings never failed to lift her spirit in return.

And at twilight when stars emerged winking cold and white on deep blue velvet, she would sit upon her grassy hill wrapped snugly in woollen blankets to meditatively survey the dark forest transitioning slowly into slumber below her. Watching and waiting patiently for the coming winter, her heart filled with hope.

As the harvest season reached its zenith, Farrah felt imbued with the fiery energy of the autumn woodlands ablaze around her. She delighted in gathering armfuls of glossy scarlet leaves to toss joyfully into the open air, bare feet crunching through piles of acorns and pecans. Though winter loomed, beauty was everywhere.

Each dawn brought Farrah dancing through her garden's frosted aisles, humming in harmony with the robins and chickadees greeting the rising sun beside her. The crystalline mist of her breath in the morning air filled her spirit with childlike exhilaration. The world felt new and vibrant with each passing day's gifts waiting to be unwrapped.

Many hours were then happily lost rambling the forest paths with trusted friends, sunlight dappling through the jewelled canopy overhead. They foraged baskets brimming with wild berries, edible mushrooms and seed pods from sassafra branches while reminiscing and relishing the poetry of rebirth's passing. Togetherness fostered awe.

As dusk's rosy light infused the treetops each evening, Farrah would lead the group back home, where a bonfire already crackled invitingly in the village square. They would recount stories and sing songs together late into the night as wood smoke ribboned skyward carrying with it their soaring harmonies. Season's cycles turned but their bonds endured.

Before retiring to her warm bed each night, Farrah made sure to reflect on what beauty the day had revealed to her - leaves underfoot quilting the forest floor in myriad hues, the comforting scents of mulled cider and hearth baking, the innocent wisdom in a child's whispered secret. Each was a precious ephemeral gift to be consciously cherished.

At the harvest's bittersweet finale, as mellow autumn days hardened into early winter, Farrah's heart overflowed with gratitude for the circle revealed - what long seasons of darkness had cultivated, the light eventually harvested. She turned now without hesitance to face the coming winter chill, spirit ablaze.

As the days grew shorter and chillier with winter's gradual approach, Farrah found herself reflecting often on the immense gratitude she held in her heart for the community of loved ones surrounding her. Through even her lowest seasons, they had remained by her side, a testament to life's resilience.

On brisk mornings rimmed with frost, she would arise with the pale dawn light and assemble baskets brimming with gifts - spiced preserves canned from the last harvest, knitted scarves and mittens, still-warm loaves of zucchini bread. Farrah would then set off through the slumbering village bestowing her offerings on every doorstep she passed, feeling warmth well up inside at the imagined smiles they'd bring once the residents awoke.

Later, steam would rise from soapy buckets and worn scrub brushes outside each cottage as Farrah arrived to help her elderly neighbours with chores in preparation for winter. She raked brittle leaves, stacked firewood and sealed holes and cracks from creeping drafts. The work felt centring and purposeful, her cheerful chatter easing their isolation.

As the first flakes began to fall, hushing the land overnight in a crystallized blanket of white, Farrah woke early feeling a sense of tranquil peace settle upon her spirit. She had always quietly loved the winter season, but now its stark beauty held layered meaning after all she had endured.

She prepared to tamp down winding pathways connecting each home before the inhabitants even stirred. She imagined them opening their doors that morning to find her small gift of easier passage through the unblemished expanse ahead.

In the evenings, cottages glowed from within, candles flickering in the windows in memory of the coming solstice that turned the slow wheel remorselessly towards longer days again. Drawn by their amber warmth, Farrah brought baskets of baked goods to share over mugs of wassail and elderflower wine that loosened tongues and laughter. The gifts of darkness were hope and communion.

At night, Farrah returned home overflowing with weary contentment. She wrote sincerely in her journal of the light she now glimpsed shining from even the longest shadows - generosity kindled against brisk odds, poetry written over years in wrinkles by firelight, each small unfurling fern come spring. These lights made the darkness sacred and never without purpose.

Even as the nights stretched on into snow-muted mornings, the solstice approached, a tide of light gathering slowly beneath the silence, soon to break at last across the inky heavens. Cocooned in the warmth of community that amplified her own inner glow, Farrah turned without fear to welcome winter again.

Each morning as she meditated by her window with a steaming cup of ginger tea, watching the crystalline flakes dance silently down against the inky predawn sky, Farrah whispered a small prayer of gratitude - for the insulating warmth of shelter, for the comforting scents of cinnamon and woodsmoke that conjured childhood contentment, for the love of those dear souls who made isolation recede even in the longest nights.

When the muffled land beyond her frosted window beckoned too strongly, Farrah would bundle herself snugly and venture out to layer more insulation over the roots of slumbering perennials. She scooped up armfuls of fresh powder to lovingly blanket her tilled vegetable beds, protecting the dormant seeds—tiny promissory lights waiting to dawn again some future spring. She tucked in the earth around her.

Soon tantalizing scents would summon her to pull fragrant loaves of bread from the rickety oven or rosy-cheeked children begging for frosted sugar cookies to decorate with sprinkles. Farrah delighted in conjuring culinary warmth and colour to brighten the short, dim days ahead. Her gifts nourished her in many ways.

As dusk fell too soon each afternoon, she would deliver bundles of split logs and kindling to those in need of more fuel to survive the bitterest nights. The grateful relief in the recipients' eyes as they clasped her little lanterns filled Farrah's heart until it overflowed into starry darkness on her long walk home.

At night she lit her hearth and wrote in her journal by firelight of unsung stars still glimmering even through the longest nights - villagers sharing precious last morsels with those in need, small hands extended without hesitation in comfort, the wisdom time's passage etches soundlessly. The light was sown even in fallow ground.

When at last the town square's great fir was set aglow with cheery paper lanterns, Farrah sang carols arm in arm with the rest, gazing up in wonder. The coming dawn drew nearer, the wheel turned slowly but inevitably. With those she loved surrounding her, Farrah felt prepared to withstand the coldest shadow. Her flame now burned within.

As the first heavy snows fell, blanketing the village overnight in a pristine veil of ivory that seemed to hush and at once amplify the slightest sound, Farrah awoke feeling a calm sense of purpose stirring within her - to bring whatever light and warmth she could to those struggling through the isolation of winter's coldest grasp.

When anxious thoughts crowded too close on a dawn's crisp air, she found peace in rituals of self-care to still her mind - rose-scented candles flickering on deep windowsills while she journaled of gratitude, preparing basins of aromatic teas brewed from dried elderflowers and rosehips. Steeping in simple nurture fostered clarity on her long road ahead.

Soon Farrah would pull on woollen layers and clomp through the frosted woods with baskets of provisions - jars of preserved late berries and honeycomb, bundles of pine kindling and mittens she had knitted through melancholy evenings. She left them hanging like precious lanterns on the door handles of those ice-locked in poverty's lonely shadow, before continuing on.

To lift the spirits of inquisitive children kept cooped up too long, Farrah would craft snow fairies in enchanted poses across the village gardens come dusk- softening day's end under their benevolent smiles. She hoped the figures offered silent assurance that even in the darkest trials, beauty waits intact beneath the still surface for those who tend its kindling.

On nights when the town nestled silently under winter's heavy quilt, friendships unfurled anew around Farrah's glowing hearth toasting wassail over mugs of rosehip tea and buttery shortbread cookies. Their voices joined in familiar carols were the simmering laughter of shared sustenance that tempered the raw chill descending outside.

Before crawling each night into her own bed's warmth, Farrah wrote sincerely in her journal of small lanterns still illuminating her long path ahead - the smell of cider infused with pine and clove, the fairy sculptures' tranquil beauty under the moonlight, chocolate melting slowly on the tongue, the gift of enduring human bonds through even the longest bitter chill. However, dim, light remained.

As the nights stretched on towards solstice, the darkest point of stillness before rebirth, Farrah felt a profound calm settle over her spirit despite the howling storms battering her little cottage from all sides. She found peace in her newfound faith that the coming dawn approached, however remote.

In preparation for celebrating that moment of returning light, Farrah would spend long, meditative hours carefully hand-copying poems or illustrations into leather journals for loved ones and stitching their names in golden thread onto hand-dyed scarves. Gifts from the heart to the heart kindled shared light.

Friends arrived rosy-cheeked on her doorstep throughout the

113

days, bearing delicacies from their own kitchens that filled hers with decadent scents - sweet potato casserole sticky from maple and pecans, spicy pear chutney, tart cranberry curd dotted with orange zest. Though simple, their tangible bonds of care sustained Farrah.

When at last the village square became adorned with glittering lanterns and boughs of holly, Farrah gathered there with the others, mittened hands clasping tightly. Together they would sing out defiantly into the cold crystalline silence, watching their collective breaths swirl upwards towards the endless stars. The sun still shone just beyond sight.

After feasting communally on hearty stews and just-baked potpies that warmed chilled fingers and bellies, the night would end with shared laughter and nostalgic reminiscences around cosy hearths glowing to push against the oppressive darkness. But it had already reached its zenith - light's return was imminent now.

Farrah focused on the symbolism of darkness giving way to light. With those she loved around her, Farrah felt prepared to weather the passing of even this storm. The sun set but also rose again - that was the covenant they would remember together. Spring would come again.

As the winter solstice passed and days slowly lengthened, Farrah felt stirrings of hope within her weary spirit. The darkness had not claimed her; she was still standing, however fragile.

Throughout the nights that followed, she found rituals to focus herself on the coming rebirth - reading poetry aloud by candlelight of the spring's eventual return, preparing tiny satchels with herbs and seeds to be scattered into the soil once fertile again. She planted promises of light.

Mornings were spent with the other children gathering precious stores of feathers, stones and fallen branches, their small mittened hands working industriously to craft gifts they would again bestow once greenery returned. Through creativity, they kindled shared hope.

When the nights had, at last, reached their zenith, Farrah slept soundly, the rhythmic sound of snowflakes kissing the icy ground outside her window oddly comforting now. The darkness could not rage much longer. Winter solstice had passed. The slow wheel was turning inevitably towards warming light again.

In the mornings after solstice had passed into lengthening light, Farrah found profound peace in simple rituals to usher in the coming spring, however far off it still seemed on the surface. She focused her meditations on the sun's slow journey northward again even as ice still clutched the land in its harsh grasp.

While pale dawn light etched intricate patterns on the frosted glass, she would wrap herself in a worn quilt by the window to journal of her gratitude for survival and hard-won wisdom - how the longest nights taught her compassion as sap slows wisely in the trees. True calm comes from embracing the cycles.

115

When she ventured out into the sleepy world, feet crunching over ice-crusted snow, she felt solace in leaving offerings along her path for wildlife also hunkered down awaiting renewal - handfuls of seeds and nuts scattered for hungry birds, tufts of wool tucked into tree hollows for chilled squirrels. She sustained those who sustained her.

Friends arrived on her doorstep with gifts of their own making - hand-pressed flower oils bottled to evoke nostalgia of summer's blossoms, braided wreaths of aromatic cedar boughs and dried orange slices to lift the spirits. Though simple, their kindness warmed her like rare sunlight through the ice.

And after each day passed, she meditated a while by flickering hearth light on the eternal promise that dawn inevitably follows the longest night. The darkness had not weakened life's resilience, merely ushered it into quieter hours of wise patience. Spring was coming. They need only hold fast a little longer.

As the days gradually and almost imperceptibly grew longer after the winter solstice had passed, Farrah found comfort in small rituals to nurture any nascent sparks of light and renewal while the land still slumbered in winter's freeze.

Mornings often found her kneeling patiently by the weak sunlight streaming onto her frosted windows, carefully turning the leaves of her houseplants so even those shadowed faces could soak up sustenance from the scant rays. She sustained their green flames until spring's bounty returned.

Donning her woollen layers, Farrah would venture out to

silently sweep clear the stoops of any still snowbound by illness or age, leaving small gifts on their steps - jars of savoury bone broth simmered overnight, braided wreaths of aromatic cedar, pinecones dipped in beeswax and rolled in spices. Anonymity enabled her to focus solely on spreading what light she could.

Throughout the short days, she kept occupied crafting trinkets to be given come spring - carving animal figurines from blocks of pine, decorating candles with dried petals and herbs, embroidering leaves and vines onto headscarves so the beauty of the living world crowned those who wore them. She kindled future warmth and cheer through each meticulous stitch.

With wisdom, community and care, her spirit would withstand winter's fury once more. The dawn was coming.

As winter's grasp slowly relinquished, Farrah felt hope and purpose quicken within once more. The land's renewal was nearing and she turned her focus towards preparing offerings that would spread light when fragile new life emerged again.

Farrah focused on the small signs of renewal that signalled better days ahead. Gentle spring light was returning to melt the gloom away.

In the pale dawn light before venturing out, she would crush dried flower petals and leaves gathered through the autumn to mix with beeswax, lavender oil and tree resins, letting the sun's weak warmth meld their soothing scents into tapers and salves she would gift come spring.

Seeing the first green shoots poke through decaying leaves filled Farrah with hope. She pressed vibrant hellebore flowers, chronicling nature's incremental awakening.

Lighting fragrant candles and filling her cottage with fresh-cut plum blossoms brought warmth and cheer against the lingering chill. Surrounding herself with scents of rebirth lifted her mood.

Farrah spent time tidying and organizing her art supplies, readying to create again as motivation returned with spring's blossoming. Preparing for creativity fuelled optimism.

On the evenings when melancholy threatened to dim her flickering motivation again, Farrah sought solace in song - humming half-forgotten melodies from childhood as she knitted colourful socks to warm future bare feet, chanting sacred mantras passed down generations to renew her flagging spirit until she could infuse light again. Vocal rituals carried her through the starless hours.

And at the end of each passing day that brought them nearer spring's return, she listed small blessings she had overlooked in her fixation on the coming thaw - the beauty of hoarfrost etched across windowpanes by dawn's faint light, the sweet perfume of tangerines sharing their summer sun, the solace of fireside moss-stitching as the wind howled impotently outside. Even winter's greedy grasp was nurtured.

The long winter nights had cultivated an enduring inner light within Farrah. Now she turned her gaze firmly on the sun growing brighter on the horizon, ready to bloom again.

One warm spring morning, Farrah awoke to birdsong and sunshine streaming through her open window. Energy and purpose surged within her spirit. Today was a new beginning.

She dressed in a shimmering floral gown, feeling finally ready to fully embrace life again after such a long and isolating winter. No more dimming her light - it was time for bold blossoming.

Farrah breezed outside, bare feet connecting with soft mossy earth, the fresh air filling her lungs. She turned her face up to the cloudless blue sky and closed her eyes as a contented smile spread across her face.

Today she would paint again, plant her garden and visit friends who had sustained her during those interminable grey days and nights. But first, Farrah opened her arms wide, spun freely and laughed aloud from the sheer joy of being alive.

She stretched her glistening wings and took to the air, sailing high above the awakening forest. Farrah had made it through the darkest valley once more. Now her spirit shone even brighter, adorned with the wisdom winter had cultivated within.

As she danced and looped weightlessly through the fragrant spring breeze, Farrah knew she would never take simple moments of beauty or connection for granted again. Each was a miracle.

Of course, there would still be pockets of gloom ahead at times. But with hope, community and compassion learned on this journey, she could weather any future storm. For now, Farrah let her bold spirit fully take flight once more under spring's golden light.

Chapter 6: Bursting Forth with Light

As the last icy breaths of winter reluctantly surrendered their grasp, Farrah arose one dewy morning feeling her spirit kindle with the stirring of new life all around her. The land's renewal beckoned and her heart quickened to answer once more.

With the pale dawn light infusing her bedroom in a rosy glow, Farrah dressed swiftly in a jasmine-hued gown stitched with tiny pearlescent beads along the bodice - an echo of spring's first unfurling blooms. She practically skipped through her morning rituals, unable to contain the motes of light effervescing within.

Stepping outside into the silken dawn as birdsong filled the awakening forest, Farrah lifted her face skyward, letting the honeyed sunlight wash over her upturned features. She basked in its tender warmth seeping into her skin, filling her cells with replenishing light after the isolating winter chill.

After so many months of stillness, colour and fragrance now blossomed everywhere - emerald moss pushing up through rust-hued earth, ruby buds adorning the branches overhead. The land was alive and renewed. And with it, her own creative spirit now clamoured too for an outlet after its dormancy.

Unable to contain the energy buzzing through her veins, Farrah broke into an impulsive dance, whirling through patches of violets as sunlight dappled down through new leafy boughs. She waved playfully to a startled fawn peeking out from beneath its mother's watchful gaze nearby. Her crystalline laughter rang out, resounding through the sun-washed glade.

When her exuberance was somewhat tamed, Farrah alighted gracefully on a flat boulder beside the burbling creek to sketch the stirrings of life around her with charcoal on parchment - silhouettes of squirrels chasing each other up trees, birds swooping to pluck twigs for nests and a family of raccoons peeking cautiously out from their winter den, damp noses sniffing the fresh scents. The world was born anew.

Later, her wings carried Farrah drifting aimlessly from meadow to forest glen, bare feet embracing the tender shoots of new grass as she breathed deeply of nature's perfume. Up ahead, golden light filtering down through the trees spotlighted a welcome sight - Willa waving in greeting from atop a mossy log.

Farrah's heart leapt to see her dear friend had also emerged from winter's hibernation. She rushed forward to embrace Willa, feeling profound gratitude for their bond that had remained unwavering even through her darkest seasons. Without her stalwart support, the light now kindling within may have been lost forever.

Together they set off to amble through the sun-dappled glade, Farrah recounting the small wonders she had witnessed already this morning with revived eyes - the iridescent wings of a dragonfly coming to rest on her finger, dewdrops trapped like liquid crystal in a spider's web. Each sign of life renewed hers in turn.

Arm in arm, they paused often when some particular natural treasure caught their eye - a patch of tiny purple crocuses carpeting the forest floor, glossy fiddleheads poking up along the creek's banks, a delicate robin's egg fallen intact beneath its treetop nest. Miracles were everywhere again, waiting to be uncovered.

In the meadow, they joined the other young sprites lying amidst the tall grasses and wildflowers, soaking up the sunshine they had craved through the cold months. Laughter and easy chatter floated on the balmy air as they wove daisy chains and plucked dandelions to wish on.

Farrah's heart swelled being immersed in such lightness again after her isolation. These simple pleasures of the sun on her skin, friends reunited and the earth's offerings suddenly abundant seemed infinitely precious now. She had emerged weathered from the chill but bursting aglow once more.

The next morning, Farrah awoke feeling as though rays of sunshine were already streaming through her heart. The unbridled joy and enthusiasm of yesterday still flowed through her spirit today.

After breakfast, she fluttered outside into the golden daylight and giggled as a breeze danced through her hair and wings. It was a perfect day for spreading more smiles and laughter.

Farrah began by picking a vibrant bouquet of wildflowers - oxeye daisies, purple asters, goldenrods. She delivered them to the local bakery along with a jar of fresh honey from her apiary.

The bakers beamed at the gifts to brighten their kitchen.

Next, Farrah visited Edgar as he was sorting through baskets of wildflowers and herbs for his potions. An impish idea struck her and soon she was tossing handfuls of petals over his head as he laughed.

Later, while strolling through the village square, Farrah spotted a father trying to teach his young pixie son to fly. She helped cheer the anxious fledgling on until he was successfully airborne, giggling with glee.

At day's end, Farrah's cheeks were sore from smiling so much. But it was a fulfilling sort of weariness. With constant compassion and care, her inner light was now able to shine freely and brightly again, bringing joy to so many lives.

Over the next few weeks, Farrah felt her natural exuberance and playfulness steadily returning now that the heavy fog had lifted from her spirit. Bringing small acts of light and laughter into others' days filled her with profound satisfaction.

In the blissful weeks that followed, Farrah delighted in nurturing her creativity again after such a protracted drought. She had forgotten the sense of peace and fulfilment that came from crafting beauty into the world through her hands. But now inspiration flowed freely once more.

Mornings often found her happily gardening until sweat dewed her sun-kissed brow - carefully transferring seedlings outdoors to acclimate, pinching back herbs for fuller growth and tidying withered foliage to make room for new life. She murmured affectionately to each tiny shoot unfurling under her diligent care.

Later when the day's heat reached its peak, Farrah would retreat indoors to weave vibrant wall hangings from strands of dyed wool, paint delicate watercolours depicting nature's seasonal renewal, or craft elaborate floral wreaths from foliage, blooms and seed pods gathered on her ambles. She created both to nourish her spirit and spread joy.

Friends were eager beneficiaries, arriving on Farrah's doorstep with gratitude shining in their eyes to gently receive her latest offerings - strawberry cheesecakes crowned with blossoms from her garden, hand-embroidered tunics patterned with exotic birds and vines, jars of meadowsweet-scented body balm to refresh parched winter skin. Each gift reflected some small fragment of beauty she had gathered from the natural world around her and distilled into a new form. And in so doing, she multiplied loveliness.

When restlessness beckoned her outside again as it often did, Farrah would ramble barefoot through wildflower meadows with an easel and paints in tow, settling in a different picturesque landscape each day to capture its unique splendour. Glazing rich oils over the textured canvas to recreate a sunset's blazing vermillion glow or dew-kissed buds unfurling along a vine connected her profoundly to life's canvas.

As the weeks went by, Farrah felt herself truly coming alive again after such a long slumber. Now that her inner light was unburdened, she delighted in playing tricks and bringing laughter everywhere she went.

Each morning Farrah awoke tingling with ideas for spreading joy and amusement through the village. She left acorns for Edgar to find by filling his boots with them, hid Maya's favourite cookies in odd spots, pretended to read Willa's palm and make up ridiculous predictions.

Everyone remarked on how wonderful it was to see Farrah's mischievous and creative spirit renewed. Her unique gifts had been sorely missed, though no one had wanted to pressure her before she was ready.

But now Farrah radiated pure enthusiasm and levity. The fog that had muted her world for so long seemed a distant memory. Seeing smiles light up loved ones' faces when she made their days more magical brought Farrah deep fulfilment.

Some nights, Farrah and the pixies gathered at the meadow's edge to release swarms of enchanted fireflies, dancing joyfully together under the twinkling lights. Laughter and wonder emanated from their circle deep into the night.

By spreading her gifts freely again, Farrah sensed she had truly rediscovered her purpose. And it was even sweeter now for having been absent awhile. She felt blessed to give and receive so much joy.

As spring shifted into gilded summer days, Farrah felt the warm renewal surrounding her seep into her bones, leaving her spirit illuminated from within with restless inspiration. After enduring winter's scouring, she now sought to live each moment awash fully in beauty and purpose once more.

Mornings often drew Farrah outdoors early to gather armfuls of velvety peonies, blowsy roses and confident sunflowers from her garden while still kissed with dew. She would fashion the cut blooms into bouquets to be spontaneously gifted, eliciting delighted surprise when recipients opened their doors to discover her offerings nestled there.

The sun-washed days passed in a blissful flurry of creativity for Farrah - drawing fantastical forest creatures with coloured pencils, teaching herself to play lively folk songs on the hand-carved lap harp gifted by a local woodworker and baking blackberry pies cradled in lattice crusts to share with loved ones while still warm. She felt truly herself again.

Evenings were reserved for meandering barefoot through meadows sprinkled with wildflowers as fireflies began to swirl through the violet dusk. There Farrah would meet with those few trusted confidantes who had remained by her side even through the darkest winters. They would exchange stories of their growth with eyes aglow in the deepening twilight until night unfurled its inky canvas above, dusted all over with stars.

Before drifting off to sleep each night with windows flung open to welcome in the sweet summer air, Farrah's heart overflowed with gratitude - for the beauty surrounding her every moment, for the bonds of others that amplified her inner light, for the wisdom and empathy the difficult seasons had etched into the fibre of her being. She had emerged renewed and ablaze.

As summer reached its zenith, the energy thrumming through the emerald land felt to Farrah as if it was streaming into her too from all sides - sunlight filling her bones, scents of honeysuckle and grass imbuing her cells, birdsong reverberating through her spirit. She sought to transpose this living tapestry into her own unique creative impressions.

Morning's rosy glow often found her sitting atop the grassy cliff overlooking the mist-wreathed valley, sketching the gradual awakening of the world below in watery pastels - smudged lines slowly clarifying into trees, rooftops, threads of smoke from early risers kindling morning fires. Her art brimmed with nostalgia for life's inevitability.

On the hottest afternoons, Farrah wandered slowly through sultry, buzzing meadows nearby to gather delicacies - wild raspberries warm from the sunshine, chamomile flowers at their peak potency and handfuls of succulent purslanes to be stirred into cool evening salads. She curated for others' taste buds treats that immersed one fully in summer's essence.

At dusk when the fireflies emerged, Farrah ferried covered baskets brimming with her harvestings to share at impromptu gatherings in the forest clearings or atop grassy hillocks under the darkening sky. There everyone would feast leisurely, laughing together and singing old folk songs until the inky heavens glittered all over with stars. Life's simplicity and community were soul food.

And at the end of each day, as she finally lay atop her sheets damp with humidity, listening to crickets trilling just outside her open window, Farrah's spirit felt immersed completely in the present's tender magnificence. Just as she had learned to honour winter's dark nourishment, now she drank in the light she had emerged into with profound wonder and gratitude for life's resilience. The soil had grown rich.

The land's feverish fertility slowly mellowed into autumn's more introspective energy, leaves fading from emerald towers into jewelled flames as the angle of light shifted. But Farrah nurtured the gifts of each passing season, honouring the fullness of existence in all its textures.

Mornings were celebrated with meandering walks alone through forests transformed overnight into vivid palettes of ruby, garnet and topaz. The melody of leaves drifting down around her was meditation and poetry, releasing attachment to the fleeting. She would lean against massive oak trunks and weep in sheer awe of impermanence.

The shortening afternoons were reserved for gathering nature's bounty from the harvest while it abounded - baskets of fuzz-pelted pears, woven wreaths of bronze chrysanthemums and marigolds, jars of jewel-toned blackberry and elderberry preserves glowing like stained glass on her pantry shelves. Out of death, so much fecundity and richness of spirit.

At twilight, as the stars emerged winking one by one, Farrah welcomed friends to gatherings on her grassy hillside, tucked snugly under woollen blankets with steaming mugs of cider.

Together they would share in the communal melancholy and nostalgia that came with summer's passing, released through stories, songs and comfortable silences. But they knew rebirth approached again.

As the last frosts of winter finally retreated from the land, Farrah awoke one dewy morning feeling energy rippling through her spirit. The sun's tender warmth seeping through her window filled her with anticipation - today was a day for rebirth.

She dressed swiftly in a shimmering gown the hopeful green of new buds. Outside her door, a few tiny purple crocuses now peeked through the earth, signalling spring's arrival. Farrah paused to gently stroke their silken petals, overwhelmed with gratitude. This bleak season too had passed.

Farrah closed her eyes, unfurling her wings slowly after months tucked away. She gave them an experimental flap, then began spinning faster until her feet lifted off the ground. Joyful laughter rang out as she twirled weightlessly through the crisp morning air. How she had missed this feeling!

Eventually alighted in a sunny meadow now dotted with wildflowers. She settled amidst the grasses and breathed deeply, allowing the balmy breeze to caress her skin. Nearby, Willa waved eagerly from atop a mossy log.

"Farrah!" she called. "Come, we're all gathering to celebrate the changing seasons!"

Smiling, Farrah rushed over to embrace her dear friend. Willa had stayed steadfast by her side even through the darkest winters. Now they would delight in springtime's arrival together.

The two friends made their way through the meadow, joining the lively group of sprites already chasing each other between the trees. Someone had set up an outdoor picnic beneath the dogwoods, replete with honey cakes and wild strawberries.

Musicians plucked lively melodies on hand-carved flutes and fiddles as pixies bedecked themselves in garlands of fresh blossoms. The very air buzzed with vitality. Farrah's heart swelled being immersed in such collective joy again after her long malaise.

Later, bellies full of treats and spirits lifted by the impromptu celebration, Farrah and Willa wandered slowly back through the forest. They paused often to admire the details of nature's renewal around them - fuzzy pussy willows, tender new ferns uncurling, proud trilliums spotting the meadows.

"Remember how we used to play hide and seek among the wildflowers when we were young?" Willa asked with a playful smile.

Farrah grinned. "I'd love that."

Laughing like sprites again, they spent the rest of the afternoon darting amidst the blooms, leaving only rumpled grass and scattered petals in their wake. It felt so wonderful to set worries aside and simply play.

That evening, Farrah returned home floating on air. Her heart was full of uncomplicated joy again after such a desolate winter. The land was reborn and with it, her childlike wonder. She fell asleep dreaming of the brightness still to come.

Whenever she had the energy, Farrah would gather friends at night for communal meals, music and poetry readings under candlelight. Seeing bonds deepen through creativity and conversation filled her heart to the brim.

Now that her inner flame was unburdened, Farrah found meaning in the simplest joys - pinecones blanketed in snow, icicles glittering in dawn's light, the innocence of children unleashing their imaginations. Each moment was a gift to be cherished.

In the blissful weeks that followed the arrival of spring, Farrah felt creative inspiration gradually returning to her long-parched spirit. She spent her days manifesting beauty through rediscovered artistic gifts that soothed her soul.

Most mornings, she tended her herb garden still vibrant with blossoms - pinching back leaves for cooking, harvesting cheerful calendulas to infuse in skin balms and deadheading spent blooms to make room for new buds. Working with her hands on the soft earth brought peace.

On cooler afternoons, Farrah retreated indoors to paint. Having gathered an armful of wildflowers - foxgloves, poppies, cornflowers - she spent hours recreating their vivid chaos on canvas. Losing herself in vivid vermilions and sapphires reignited a sense of flow within.

On other days, she foraged for windfall tree branches and carved whimsical forest creatures from the smooth wood - owls, rabbits, turtles. Gifting the finished pieces around the village spread the delight she felt in crafting. Each creation nurtured the spark within.

Evenings were reserved for quiet cups of chamomile tea on her porch, watching fireflies begin to swirl as dusk fell. Listening to the ringing chorus of frogs and crickets from the nearby creek soothed her lingering melancholy. The land was alive again and so was she.

When she got nostalgic, Farrah would sneak honey cakes into Willa's pocket when she wasn't looking, just like when they were young. Willa would pretend to scold her later through giggles.

At night, Farrah would reflect in her journal on the multitude of gifts she had been given - unwavering friendship, the beauty of nature and opportunities to spread light each day. With deep gratitude, she looked brightly at the road ahead.

As spring flourished into full bloom, so did Farrah's spirit. She had not felt this buoyant and optimistic in ages. Now her days were filled with laughter, sunshine and possibilities.

Each morning, Farrah awoke energized and eager to nurture

the simple joys she had gained an appreciation for during her time in the valley - flowers unfurling, baby birds chirping, friendly smiles passing her way.

Often, she would surprise Willa and Edgar with spontaneous picnics by the creek, complete with delicious treats and music from her harp. Turning an ordinary day into a celebration filled Farrah with delight.

The young pixies loved when Farrah would lead them on adventures through lush meadows or organize games of hide-and-seek among the orchards. Her playful spirit was infectious, lifting everyone.

Some evenings, Farrah hosted firefly dances under the stars for friends and villagers. As the shimmering bugs swirled around them, they would weave flower crowns and sing and feast on blackberry tarts late into the night.

With darkness now firmly in her past, Farrah embraced her purpose of spreading light through boundless generosity, creativity and love. She had emerged wiser, with joy that radiated outward touching every life she encountered.

As spring shifted into gilded summer days, Farrah felt infused with the energy and splendour of the season. She had not felt this carefree and alive in years. Every moment was a gift to be savoured.

Each morning she awoke singing, fresh ideas already filling her head for how to spread joy and laughter through the village.

Farrah wanted everyone to share in the delight that bubbled up within her spirit now.

Mornings were still dedicated to tending her garden, now overflowing with ripe tomatoes, plump squash, fragrant herbs and cheerful zinnias. Farrah often arose before dawn to water and weed in the cool air before harvest time.

Often, she would pick wild daisies and weave them into necklaces and crowns to gift the young pixie children, who would then dance around looking like fairy kings and queens. Their innocence and zeal brought Farrah pure happiness.

On sunny afternoons, she would gather friends in the meadow for games, music and feasts of plump berries under the boundless blue sky. Edgar played lively flute melodies as everyone laughing twirled hand in hand.

Some days Farrah simply soared alone through the crisp air, looping and diving over verdant forests, cool rivers and quaint villages nestled amongst the hills. Each sight filled her heart to bursting with uncomplicated joy.

By night, snuggled in bed with a contented smile, Farrah knew that after every valley came a new spring. Her light now shone brighter and bolder than ever before, illuminating all the vibrant possibilities ahead.

As summer reached its zenith, so too did Farrah's spirit. She had not felt such hope and vitality in years. The world seemed new and vibrant again after emerging from her long cocoon of isolation.

Now Farrah awoke each morning with childlike excitement for the day ahead. She would sing whilst getting dressed and eat her breakfast on her porch, watching the bustle of villagers starting their days too.

On the hottest mornings, she arose with the dawn to gather dew-kissed flowers and herbs from her garden before the sun grew too intense. Bouquets of black-eyed susans, sunflowers and fragrant lavender adorned every room of her cottage.

In the afternoons, she could be found down by the creek, bare feet dipped in cool water, while she wove flower crowns with the pixies or helped them float leaf boats downstream. Laughter rang out frequently in her presence.

On other days Farrah would simply wander through meadows abloom with wildflowers, breathing in their sweet scents, making wishes on dandelions gone to seed. She saw miracles everywhere again in nature's details.

At night, Farrah would release swarms of fireflies from her cupped palms and watch their flickering lights drift into the inky sky. Everything felt new and magical once more.

Her inner flame, which had nearly extinguished during those cold periods of gloom, now burned bold and bright, nurtured by a community that cherished her unique spirit.

As the bountiful summer days eventually softened into autumn,

Farrah marvelled at the beauty of the changing seasons. She appreciated the quiet wisdom of winter now, knowing it made spring's rebirth so meaningful.

The difficult seasons had carved channels within her spirit allowing joy to flow freely once more. Now Farrah embodied summer's essence - boldly creative, deeply connected, perpetually in awe of nature's abundance. She had emerged into the light again.

Each morning as she walked, Farrah would crunch through piles of golden leaves, remembering when she had once rushed by them blindly, too lost in gloom. Now she saw and felt it all - life's texture and brilliance.

Farrah spent many afternoons showing the pixies how to preserve summer's harvest for the coming colder months. They worked together canning peaches and berries, drying fragrant herbs and bottling juices from ripe fruit. Keeping busy brought Farrah calm purpose.

When she needed solitude, Farrah would collect acorns and colourful leaves to fashion mosaic art, or write poetry under oak trees by the creek. She cherished reconnecting with her lost creativity.

Before cocooning each night in quilted blankets with her window ajar to welcome in autumn's loamy scents, Farrah would reflect in her journal on all she had gained from walking through the darkness - wisdom, resilience, deepened empathy and joy. Without hardship, life's beauty could not shine so brilliantly. She was eternally grateful for this rediscovered light.

As the harvest season reached its peak, Farrah felt immense gratitude for the simple gifts in her life now - friends who felt like family, the changing trees blazing with colour and hearty home-cooked meals shared by the fire. She had learned not to take any of it for granted.

Each morning brought fresh inspiration for projects - baking pumpkin bread and delivering it warm to neighbours, embroidering woollen scarves for the pixies and crafting corn husk dolls as mantel decorations. Keeping her hands busy nourished Farrah's soul.

On clearer days, she would lead friends on meandering hikes through the forest to forage for wild mushrooms and come upon hidden grottos blanketed in moss. Exploring new pockets of beauty brought them closer.

At night, Farrah would build a bonfire in her yard and invite loved ones over to roast apples and nuts, tell stories and sing songs until the glowing embers faded. Their community and laughter warmed her from within.

In all of life's colourful textures, from the crunch of leaves underfoot to the flickering candle flames on her windowsill, Farrah now saw quiet miracles she had overlooked in her past gloom. But her vision was forever clear now - she knew this light was eternal.

As the harvest season came to a close, Farrah spent more time quietly reflecting on all she had endured getting here - where crimson leaves and cosy hearth fires filled her heart with indescribable gratitude. She was not the same fairy as before the darkness.

Now in everything - the copper kettles hanging in Willa's kitchen, the rustle of animals preparing for winter, the neighbourly smiles passing her way - Farrah saw beauty. Each was a precious gift to be cherished, for she understood how fleeting it all could be.

When melancholy still visited, as it likely always would, Farrah had strategies to care for herself - hot baths, poetry, imagining the coming spring. She knew the light always returned with time and self-compassion.

Laughter came easily now, spilling out like sunbeams after being muted for so long. Seeing the wrinkles form around Willa's eyes as she chuckled warmed Farrah's heart like nothing else. This was her purpose.

As dusk fell earlier each night, Farrah would light the oil lamps lining her windows, sending beacons of hope out into the darkness. For those still adrift, may you find your way too, she wished them.

Her inner flame had been tested ruthlessly by winter's fury but emerged radiant. Now Farrah felt prepared to weather any future storms - with wisdom, community and the certain knowledge that spring always comes, no matter how long the night.

As the last golden leaves spiralled down and the first snows fell blanketing the forest, Farrah awoke feeling a sense of peace and gratitude that this winter would be different. Her spirit was nourished now, her inner hearth fire burning steadily after being rekindled through so much darkness.

Each morning, she rose with the sun's first light and stood gazing out her frosty window, sipping cinnamon tea. Farrah whispered blessings for all who would struggle this isolating season - may you know you are loved.

When melancholy came, she turned inward through meditation, journaling and listening to the quiet. But when motivation flowed, Farrah showered loved ones with care – home-baked cookies, handwritten poetry and little trinkets that reminded her of them.

Seeing the pixies' frozen noses and ruddy cheeks as they bundled up to make snow fairies filled Farrah with tenderness. Their bright spirits through winter's fury never ceased to inspire her own.

At night, safe beneath her down quilt as the wind howled outside, Farrah's heart swelled with love for this imperfect but beautiful existence. Once she had wanted to dim her light forever, but now - now she would nurture its glow for all to see.

As winter deepened, Farrah cherished the opportunity to

reflect and prepare mentally for the coming spring. She knew from experience now that this season of stillness and melancholy was an important part of nature's cycle too.

Baking sweet breads kneaded her anxiety away while delivering the loaves letting her spread warmth through the isolated village. Seeing hearts lifted kept Farrah's own spirit glowing steadily through the bitter nights.

As the solstice neared, Farrah strung paper lanterns with symbols of cherished memories and hopes for the future. She knew the light still shone within, even in the darkest hour of the year, if she nurtured its fragile flame.

On long snowy days, Farrah often ventured into the Narnia-like Forest, following deer tracks through the blank canvas. The muffled silence and scent of woodsmoke in the air filled her with tranquil nostalgia. Even in sadness, so much beauty awaited eyes opened to receive it.

As winter deepened, Farrah withdrew more each day - from the land around her and within herself. But this time she did not fear the darkness. She meditated, wrote and rested, knowing spring would come again in time. Patience and faith were learned through the cycling seasons.

The bitterest nights were still wounded, but she focused on small comforts - the warmth of a crackling fire, cinnamon mingling with pine on her festive garlands, friendships like evergreen boughs, sturdy and steadfast through howling storms. These lights led the way until dawn returned.

143

Soon the sun's radiance would return to bathe her spirit anew. But for now, Farrah focused on mining the gifts of winter's darkness - resilience, creativity and purified joy. Spring would come again and she would be ready.

As winter's chill gradually relinquished to emerging signs of spring, Farrah reflected on how much the seasons mirrored her own inner cycles of light and darkness. She had emerged wiser from the harshness and isolation.

Now she welcomed each morning with ritual and intent - watching the newly etched sunrise while drinking ginger tea infused with optimism, writing three things she was grateful for and planning small acts of kindness to manifest.

The future no longer intimidated Farrah as it once had. She understood now that though fallow periods would come, she possessed the inner light to nourish herself through until joy bloomed again.

Farrah spent many days with friends preparing their gardens for spring planting. Turning over the soil, nurturing seedlings and envisioning future bounty brought her profound peace after winter's dearth. This was the work of hope.

At night, Farrah would reflect in her journal on personal seeds she wanted to cultivate in the coming months too - trying new creative pursuits, travelling to inspiring places, penning her story to provide others light.

With time and care, the most beautiful gardens could grow

from even the most hardened ground. She was proof of that. Soon Farrah would bloom fully once more, turned boldly toward the sun.

As the last frosts retreated and spring blossomed, Farrah felt her spirit lifting along with the greening earth. The bitter isolation of winter was receding, new light was infusing the land once more.

Now she awoke singing, throwing open her shutters to welcome in birdsong and sweet floral scents. Farrah would dance around her room watering seedlings on the sill that would soon adorn her garden.

Often, she wandered misty forests simply noticing beauty reemerging. Hidden waterfalls now gurgled with meltwater, moss glowed impossibly green and tiny buds on bare branches promised wonders to come.

Farrah spent many days with the pixies planning playful springtime mischief - daisy chain secret passageways, leaf boat regattas, searching for fairy rings and other natural magic. Life was meant for joy.

At night, she would build bonfires in her yard and all her friends would come feast, sing and dance beneath the stars like they used to do. Their laughter rang out louder than ever after such muted seasons.

As Farrah stood with her face upturned to the golden spring sun, she knew she had bloomed through the long cold night.

Her heart had been tested, but now love flowed freely once more. She was alive again.

As spring flourished into summer, every fibre of Farrah's being felt illuminated with purpose and possibility. She embraced the busy energy of the fertile seasons, soaking up the sunshine and nearness of the community.

Each morning brought fresh inspiration - places in the valley to explore, creative projects to begin, wildflowers to press and pies to bake for loved ones. Farrah cherished staying immersed in nurturing beauty and joy.

Often, she could be found sitting cross-legged on the sun-warmed earth, assembling flower crowns with the pixie children as they chattered happily around her. Their innocence filled her with hope.

On balmy evenings, fireflies rose over the meadow as friends gathered to release floating paper lanterns on the creek and weave tales of renewed dreams. Laughter and promises filled the air until they all fell asleep beneath the stars.

At summer's peak, everything felt immersed in magic - jewelled dragonflies, sweet berry picking, moonlit swims, the feeling of grass under bare feet. Farrah's heart overflowed with gratitude to be alive.

The wheel turned and darkness became light once more. Now Farrah danced freely in the sun's radiance, spread wings and spirit finally unfurled. She was blooming fully again, bold and vibrant as ever before.

As the bountiful summer days eventually softened into autumn, Farrah was reminded of her inward seasons of darkness transforming into light. She now saw the wisdom in times of dormancy and emergence.

Each morning brought fresh motivation - gathering acorns and leaves, canning summer produce and decorating her cottage with pinecones and gourds. Keeping her hands happily busy brought Farrah calm purpose.

She loved exploring the forest paths ablaze with colour, reminiscing on seasons past but also looking ahead. The future seemed full of potential and Farrah knew she possessed the resilience to weather coming storms.

Golden afternoons were spent with friends strolling through crunchy leaves, drinking cider from the mill and dreaming up recipes for the harvest bounty they carried home in woven baskets.

Nightfall brought roaring bonfires and stargazing as they kept each other warm, playing instruments and sharing stories late into the chill evenings. Their community filled Farrah with light.

In all things, she saw beauty now - in maple seeds spiralling down, in cosy woollen blankets, in pumpkins glowing on neighbours' porches. Gratitude and wonder had transformed her spirit forever.

As the harvest season came to a close, Farrah was reminded of her inward seasons of decay transforming into growth. She honoured this cycle, remembering rebirth always came after fallow periods.

Each morning she awoke with joyful reverence - stepping outside into the frosted air, slowly breathing in the sight of her breath crystallizing. These small miracles were gifts.

Farrah spent many afternoons strolling through the forest, reminiscing on the winding journey that had led her here. Though once lost in the darkness, now she emerged renewed and alight.

With loving hands, she tidied her cottage, sweeping out cobwebs and sprinkling dried lavender for the coming winter nesting. Preparing this safe space for hibernation brought calm purpose.

At dusk, she lit the oil lamps lining her windowsills to send beacons of hope out into the night for any still finding their way through the darkness. Their light too would come.

By the hearth, Farrah sank into her quilted chair, drinking cinnamon tea. She had survived the longest nights through compassion, community and the wisdom that spring always comes again. This she knew deep within her soul now.

One night as the first snow fell, Farrah sat by her frosted window sipping rosehip tea, listening to the comforting silence wrapping the forest in its cold embrace. She smiled, feeling truly at peace.

Her spirit had been tested ruthlessly through bitter seasons threatening to extinguish her inner light forever. But now, gazing out at the gentle snowfall, Farrah overflowed with gratitude for the resilient wisdom it had cultivated.

Each flake outside was a reminder of life's impermanence, beauty and final triumph over darkness. They collected serenely on the windowsill like all the small miracles Farrah now saw in existence.

Winter would come again, but never would she dread its fury like before - it was all part of the turning wheel. Inside, the glow that had been painstakingly kindled and sheltered now radiated a steady warmth to sustain her way forward.

Farrah was reminded of the sun - even on the gloomiest days it still shone brightly behind the clouds. Her inner fire had been nourished and now burned boldly, melting away any shadows still lurking.

Filled with purpose, Farrah gently blew out the flickering candle flame on her table, no longer needing its light. She would shine brightly enough on her own now, guiding others through winter's darkest nights back home to spring.

Chapter 7: Guiding Others Through the Darkness

Farrah glided slowly through the quiet winter woods, admiring how the blanket of fresh snow transformed the landscape into otherworldly beauty. Though the forest now lay dormant, she knew vibrant renewal awaited come spring.

Her spirit had weathered so much since first entering these woods - isolation, despair and seasons that threatened to smother her inner flame forever. But now Farrah emerged wiser and alight as the dormant trees strengthened through their rest.

She landed lightly in a sheltered glen and sat against the trunk of a towering oak. Farrah pulled out her journal and began reflecting on all she had gained on this profound journey back to spring. Though her dear mentor Ignitus had passed, his wisdom lingered - to share her story to light the way for others still adrift in darkness.

Firstly, the gifts of the community surrounding her, especially Willa's stalwart friendship through the darkest valleys. Creative outlets like writing, weaving and baking that had nourished her inner wells. A deeper appreciation for life's fleeting beauty. And most importantly, the knowledge that no night lasted forever.

Farrah realized how sharing these lessons hardship had carved within her, she could help guide others still adrift in the dark. If her light could spare even one fairy from the despair she had walked through, it would give renewed purpose to her long journey.

Energized by this aspiration, Farrah carefully packed away her journal and took flight once more into the silent woods. She soared over the stark winter landscape, heading for the hot springs where Ignitus had first kindled hope in her heart, buzzing with ideas for how to begin manifesting this vision.

The great phoenix was there waiting amidst the steaming waters. His golden eyes crinkled happily at Farrah's arrival. Though he had passed seasons ago, his spirit remained her guardian.

"Ignitus, I want to share my story to help others find their way too," Farrah declared breathlessly. "Will you help me light the path?"

The phoenix smiled knowingly. "I knew your gifts were needed in the world, little one. Together we will spread hope through the darkness."

Later that night, tucked into her cosy cottage as the winter wind howled outside, Farrah began drafting plans for how to create a sanctuary for the weary and guide them through darkness into the light once more.

Farrah's heart swelled hearing the mentor who had guided her spirit back to light now urge her onward to be a beacon for others. She returned home that night buzzing with ideas for how to begin manifesting this vision...

In the weeks that followed, Ignitus guided Farrah in realizing her vision. They began simply - Farrah volunteered with struggling youth, offered a listening ear to friends and made herself available to any seeking hope or help.

She also wrote honestly about her challenges and strategies in her journal, opening up dialogues with others experiencing similar struggles. Putting her journey into words helped demystify hardship.

Eventually, encouraged by Ignitus, Farrah formed a support group for those battling despair and isolation. In this safe space, she facilitated discussions, shared coping strategies and reminded attendees they were never alone.

On the darkest evenings, when all seemed bleak, Farrah would channel Ignitus' wisdom - "As I learned, you need only hold on until dawn comes again." She became a beacon guiding others home.

Farrah grew from a fairy desperately seeking light, to one who shone brightly in the darkness for others. By relighting extinguished spirits with care and compassion, she discovered her true purpose.

In the weeks after dedicating herself to guiding others through the darkness, Farrah felt her life fill with renewed meaning and direction. She drew from her own arduous journey to light the way for those still struggling.

Each morning she rose with fiery motivation, planning small

acts of compassion to manifest - delivering flowers to the elderly, donating art supplies to struggling youths and leaving encouraging notes on friends' doors. Small seeds of hope that Farrah nurtured daily.

She expanded her support group to new evenings, opening it up to any seeking solace and guidance traversing valleys that once overwhelmed her too. Farrah facilitated with empathy, patience and wisdom.

When members relapsed into isolation, she would visit them bearing gifts - lanterns ignited with her resilient light to illuminate their way until they could rekindle their inner flames again. Farrah knew darkness intimately but saw their strength shine through.

Some weary nights still pressed heavily, but recalling those she had helped so far reignited Farrah's motivation. Kindness multiplied exponentially, she realized - each light she nurtured sparked others.

Ignitus observed proudly as Farrah increasingly illuminated her corner of the world. "You have realized your purpose," he told her. "Now let your spirit blaze brightly to kindle endless lights beyond."

In the months that followed, word spread quickly of the sanctuary Farrah had created for those struggling with gloom and isolation. More and more travelled great distances hoping to ignite their depleted spirits with her compassion.

Farrah worked diligently to transform her cosy cottage into a sanctuary for those struggling with the type of isolation and despair she knew all too well.

She tidied every corner, letting sunlight stream in through the freshly scrubbed windows. Vases of dried lavender and rustic lanterns Created warm, welcoming touches. Herbs hung to dry from the rafters, infusing the rooms with a calming aroma.

Farrah furnished a row of guest rooms with thick handmade quilts and vases of fresh wildflowers. She filled the shelves with books of poetry, nature journals and baskets of art supplies to kindle creativity. Each room felt like a serene retreat.

In the kitchen, Farrah was careful to keep the pantry stocked with soul-nourishing ingredients - grains, dried fruit, healing herbs, jars of honey. She practised baking comforting sweets like cinnamon raisin bread to serve weary travellers. Food was medicine.

As dusk fell each night, Farrah would light the dozens of candles throughout the cottage, envisioning their flames as beacons calling out to guide lost souls back home. Soon this sanctuary would provide the rest and care she had once desperately needed.

When all was ready, Farrah finally opened her doors, letting word spread organically to nearby villages of a safe haven for those battered in body and spirit. At first, just a few curious visitors arrived. But soon more came seeking the light they had heard glowed within.

Arriving weary travellers were first welcomed into Farrah's cosy cottage and offered restorative meals of stew, medicinal tea and freshly baked bread to start mending physical fatigue. Being nourished in body, mind and soul was the first step in their journey back to light.

When they were ready, Farrah would provide new arrivals heartfelt support through group discussions or individual counselling sessions. She shared her own story and strategies that had carried her through the darkness.

Later, Farrah encouraged those recovering to pour their experiences into creative pursuits like writing, music and art. She knew firsthand the deep healing power of channelling emotions into creation.

On the toughest nights when hope felt far away, Farrah would lead visualizations, reminding her charges of their inner light waiting to reignite. And she shared Ignitus' wisdom that dawn would come again.

With every spirit revived, Farrah's glow intensified, along with her commitment to guide more out of the shadows. She had found her purpose in relighting the sparks within others that hardship had dimmed but never extinguished.

By spring, dozens of weary souls had found their way to Farrah's sanctuary, emerging renewed from their stay - spirits lighter, inner wells beginning to fill again. Watching them blossom gave Farrah hope. Her purpose had been realised, lighting the way forward for others still lost in the dark.

As word continued to spread, more visitors found their way to Farrah's sanctuary seeking solace. Each soul arrived weary but left a little brighter for the care they had received.

When new guests arrived, Farrah first showed them the cosy rooms she had lovingly prepared with thick quilts, fresh flowers and notes of encouragement. She wanted them to feel safe and cared for.

One young elf named Iris came stumbling out of the woods after months alone in despair. She had lost her dearest love and with it, her sense of hope and purpose. At first, Iris isolated herself in her guest room, speaking to no one.

But Farrah gently coaxed her to the kitchen to decorate sugar cookies together. Iris stayed silent as she carefully piped icing in pastel flowers and birds. The simple act of creating beauty started thawing the ice around her heart.

Soon Iris joined in with group craft sessions, kneading fragrant herb dough for bread, sewing quilted blankets for other guests and painting vivid watercolors of scenes from her happier days. Each small act of creation brought some light back into her vacant eyes.

By the time Iris departed the sanctuary a few weeks later, she embraced Farrah in a tight hug. "You've given me the tools to make it through this darkness," Iris said. "Now I can start to find joy and purpose again."

Watching her disappear down the forest path, Farrah's eyes

misted with bittersweet tears. But her heart swelled knowing she had helped fan Iris's inner spark from fragile embers back into a steady flame once more.

Another frequent visitor was a sprite named Jasper who struggled with anxious spells that could be paralyzing. In his first days at the sanctuary, he hardly left his room.

Farrah gently encouraged him to join short garden walks to notice birds and buds awakening with the spring. Their quiet presence eased his racing thoughts.

Gradually, Jasper felt comfortable joining the lively community meals where conversations flowed naturally. Connecting with others who had faced similar struggles helped assuage his isolation. He learned he was not alone.

The day Jasper departed, he turned back once outside the woods to wave excitedly at Farrah. Though she knew he still had inner demons to battle, he now had the tools and belief to take each day as it came.

Watching Jasper disappear stronger than he had arrived, Farrah was reminded of tiny forest flowers, often hidden but continuing to bloom every year without fail. With care and light, nothing was ever fully lost.

As Farrah's reputation as a guide through darkness spread, more weary souls arrived seeking the light they had heard glowed within her sanctuary's walls. She warmly welcomed them all.

One frequent visitor was a skeletal wraith named Raven who had fallen into deep despair after losing her forest home in a terrible fire. In the beginning, Raven isolated herself, refusing meals or activities with others.

But Farrah gently encouraged her by bringing art supplies to her room and suggesting she express her tumultuous emotions through creativity. Raven began pouring her trauma into ominous charcoal drawings filled with phantasmal shapes and clutching darkness. The release unlocked something within.

Gradually Raven joined the group quilting sessions, finding solace in stitching fabric fragments into something beautiful and whole again. Sharing stories with others whose spirits were also scarred and rebuilding kindled a sense of hope.

The day Raven departed the sanctuary, her head was held high and her eyes shone brightly. She gifted Farrah a lush dreamscape painting and promised to write soon. Watching her go, Farrah knew Raven's inner light had been stoked from frail coals back into a steady blaze once more.

Another arrival was a gaunt fairy named Wren who had fallen into a state of deep melancholy that left him listless in bed day and night. Farrah started by bringing Wren simple nourishing foods like vegetable broth and nut porridges sweetened with honey.

When he was ready, she coaxed him to short garden strolls pointing out new buds and other signs of beauty and rebirth. Slowly Wren's hollow eyes began to fill with appreciation for the living world around him again.

With Farrah's gentle encouragement, he found soothing comfort in journaling by the creek, capturing his feelings in verse and playing soft lute melodies from his childhood. Each creative act re-ignited lost parts of his spirit.

The change in Wren when he departed the sanctuary was palpable - he moved with purpose, spoke up in conversation and embraced Farrah warmly, thanking her for rekindling his inner flame when he had lost sight of it in the darkness.

Watching Wren disappear down the forest path, his shoulders no longer slumped in despair, Farrah was overcome with gratitude at being able to pass on the gifts that had once saved her. She had found her purpose lighting the way for other souls still wandering lost in the shadows.

As the weeks went on, Farrah was kept busy tending to the growing number of weary souls finding refuge within her sanctuary's walls. She felt a profound purpose illuminating the shadows haunting those who arrived seeking her help to rekindle their inner light.

One young sprite named Lily had become overwhelmed trying fruitlessly to please others until she lost touch with her own spirit's whispers. She arrived at the sanctuary feeling hollow and invisible.

Farrah slowly nurtured her back to radiance through creativity that celebrated her unique gifts - baking sweet elderflower tarts using plants Lily gathered, sewing a vibrant quilt with intricate motifs from her imagination, writing poetry late at night by candlelight in Farrah's garden. With each, she shone brighter.

The day Lily departed, she turned back with tears glistening to embrace Farrah, promising to live going forward with boldness and courage. Farrah knew Lily had found her voice again after too long spent in silent shadows.

Another arrival was a fairy named Hawthorn who had become so fearful of death after losing his partner that he clamped down on experiencing any of life. He moved mechanically through his days, unable to feel joy or sorrow.

Farrah gently encouraged him to begin letting the light back in through creative acts like gardening, music and watercolour - small steps to crack open the shell he had withdrawn into for safety. With time, Hawthorn rediscovered the capacity for not just grief but also wonder, meaning and peace.

The change in him the day Hawthorn left the sanctuary was palpable - he floated taller amongst the trees with purpose, called out cheers to fellow travellers and turned to wave at Farrah, his eyes twinkling with rekindled spirit.

Watching his shining silhouette disappear into the dappled forest, Farrah was overwhelmed with gratitude for having had the privilege to help reignite Hawthorn's diminished inner flame. She pressed on with her purpose each day.

As the seasons turned, more lost souls arrived seeking the light Farrah now shone as a beacon through the darkness. With deep empathy woven from her own unravelling and return, she nurtured them all back to radiance through compassion, creativity and care. This she knew was her life's meaning.

Farrah's humble sanctuary soon gained renown across the land as a place of respite and healing for weary souls. Fairies, elves, sprites and other woodland beings travelled from afar to seek her compassionate guidance out of isolation.

Her capacity for deep listening and sharing her own turbulent history built trust and empathy. Farrah provided refuge without judgment and nurtured visitors back to wholeness through community, creativity and care. She asked for nothing in return except their commitment to illuminate others.

One milestone was when a delegation of elven leaders sought out Farrah after hearing how she had reignited hope in their people. "You have a rare gift for piercing the darkness of even the most battered souls," they told her, presenting gifts of gratitude—finely woven tapestries depicting her good works.

Tales of Farrah's profound understanding and the way she could rekindle even the most diminished inner spark spread. Soon royal carriages arrived, bearing those of influence equally needing her wisdom. None were turned away.

After an especially harsh winter when Farrah worked tirelessly to shelter hundreds seeking her light, the sprites held a jubilant celebration honouring her unwavering compassion through the bitterest nights. "Let it be known Farrah is a beacon unto all," they declared.

Though deeply humble, Farrah was touched seeing how profoundly she had impacted so many lives. The long, winding road from her own unravelling to now guiding others had cultivated an eternal flame within her spirit. She vowed to shine on wherever darkness dwelled.

But Farrah measured her success not through accolades, but by the light reignited within weary souls seeking refuge. Watching them emerge whole, purpose restored, she knew her purpose had been fulfilled. This alone was reward enough for Farrah.

As Farrah's reputation grew, people journeyed from farther lands to seek her wisdom and compassion. However, she remained committed to nurturing each soul with the same devotion she had shown when only a few arrived.

Farrah expanded her sanctuary to welcome more of those searching for light amidst torment and isolation. She recruited a team of assistants also touched by adversity to help run the daily operations but continued directly counselling newcomers herself.

Farrah designed a self-sustaining community on the grounds - vegetable gardens, orchards, apiaries and workshops where residents could learn trades that brought them purpose again. Keeping their hands and spirits engaged in creation promoted healing.

Music and laughter rang frequently across the rolling meadows and gardens surrounding the sanctuary, signalling lives being transformed by Farrah's care. In time, many residents found the inner light to continue guiding others. They became living proof that darkness could be overcome.

In Farrah's humble kitchen, the comforting aromas of bread baking and stews simmering never ceased. She still insisted on personally helping prepare the meals, remembering her journey back from the hunger of both body and soul. Love imbued the food.

Weary newcomers arrived penniless, but none were ever turned away. Farrah provided shelter, nourishment and compassion without cost, believing she was merely returning the gifts freely given to her in times of own unravelling. Her kindness multiplied.

As seasons changed, Farrah celebrated both joys and struggles - she held space for grief in winter, led exuberant dances welcoming spring's rebirth and ignited bonfires and fireworks when darkness crested inviting light's return. Through it all, her singular purpose held true - be a candle through the night until the day dawns again.

And so Farrah's beacon burned bright, a living testament that there is no darkness that care, creativity and community cannot pierce. Those bathed in her light grew strong enough to shine for others when storms raged. She had ignited an eternal flame fending off all shadows.

As time passed, Farrah decided to compile her wisdom into a book for wider reach. She wrote honestly of her own trials through isolation and despair and the lessons life had carved into her spirit - have faith dawn follows night, seek beauty and purpose when motivation wanes and share your unique gifts however small.

Farrah's gentle memoirs captured in prose resonated with weary souls across the land. Her words brought solace and guidance to any needing to know they were not alone in the darkness. Many glowing letters arrived thanking Farrah for lighting the way forward.

Whenever she could, Farrah travelled to offer her insights in person too. She gave inspirational talks urging people to nurture community, creativity and hope amidst life's hardship. All were moved by her profound compassion borne of her own suffering.

But Farrah always returned to her tranquil sanctuary, where she could focus on nurturing each arriving soul with deep devotion. Fame interested her little - she wanted only to ease despair through the wisdom hardship's fire had forged within her. This was fulfilment enough.

As seasons turned, word of the sanctuary spread even to the ears of royalty. One day the fairy queen herself arrived unannounced and alone, her spirit battered by grief she could not defeat. Unsure of Farrah, she kept her identity hidden.

Farrah tended the queen's heart with the same gentle empathy she gave every soul. Through small creative rituals and community, the queen rediscovered inner light little by little each day. Her spirit slowly blossomed again, healed through care.

The day the queen departed, she revealed her identity and proclaimed Farrah the land's treasure. "None understand the human spirit's trials quite like you," she pronounced. "You have my eternal patronage and protection."

Farrah demurred, asking only that the queen rule with compassion and help others along her journey in return. Fame concerned her not, only the opportunity to ease suffering wherever it existed. This would be her life's meaning until the end.

So Farrah's light continued guiding people through the darkness from her tranquil sanctuary and through her writings. She asked for nothing, wanting only to give the hope that had once saved her when she thought all was lost inside her own battered spirit.

As the seasons turned, Farrah was kept busy year-round with caring for the steady influx of weary souls who made the pilgrimage to her sanctuary seeking the light they had heard emanated within.

In spring, she led visitors out into the forest to notice tiny signs of renewal that mirrored their own inner transformations - emerald buds on bare branches, fresh shoots in the meadows, morning songbirds celebrating rebirth. Farrah knew hope often hid in humble forms.

On bountiful summer days, she organized community meals in the meadows overflowing with laughter, music and storytelling beneath the stars. Farrah would recount her own winding tale, reminding them the sun always returns, even when obscured by clouds awhile.

During autumn harvests, Farrah led cranberry picking excursions and helped visitors bottle preserves to stock their pantries before winter's isolation descended. Keeping their hands productive provided comfort and purpose in the introspective season.

On winter's longest nights, she reassured shivering souls that this too would pass, encouraging them to find meaning in creating art, writing, or gathering by the fire with mugs of hot cider. Connecting through creativity turned hardship into something beautiful.

As her reputation grew, dignitaries continued to visit Farrah's humble sanctuary, seeking her wisdom. But she received each soul equally, whether pauper or prince. All were weighed down by sorrows. Her light shone for anyone searching for their way through the darkness.

Occasionally, weary again from endless caretaking, Farrah would retreat into solitude in the forest glen where her dear mentor Ignitus had first kindled hope in her spirit so long ago. There she would meditate, nourishing her soul until ready to light the way forward again.

Like the changing seasons, Farrah knew struggles would come and go. But she had ignited an eternal flame within her sanctuary that would never stop welcoming lost souls and nurturing their kindling sparks back into steady bonfires. This was her life's purpose.

So Farrah lived on as a beacon through even the longest nights, shining her light developed through suffering to illuminate the way for all who wandered lost in the wilderness. By turns, those souls grew to blaze brightly and light the darkness in others. And so her singular legacy endured.

As time passed, Farrah decided to take on an apprentice to someday carry on her important work running the sanctuary. She chose a bright young fairy named Dahlia who had recovered her inner light under Farrah's guidance.

Farrah slowly mentored Dahlia in the nuances of compassionate care - the art of deep listening while withholding judgment, gently encouraging small steps forward, community's power to banish isolation. Imparting her lifetime of wisdom to an eager student brought Farrah joy.

On days when exhaustion overwhelmed her, Farrah would send Dahlia to calmly oversee the sanctuary while she retreated into silent communion with nature, reflecting on how far she had come and all the souls she had impacted. This solitude grounded her.

When Farrah grew older and weary, she decided to live out her final days in a modest hut on the sanctuary grounds. There she could continue advising Dahlia while enjoying a slower pace, watching the fruits of her labor thrive all around her.

As seasons changed outside her window, bringing both joy and melancholy, Farrah made careful records in her journals so future generations could learn from the complex lessons life had carved into her spirit. She found peace knowing her voice would endure.

On clear nights, Farrah would build a small fire outside her hut, make chamomile tea and sit gazing up at the starry canvas of the night sky. In those quiet moments, she felt connected to the past, present and future. Her purpose had been fulfilled.

When Farrah's long, rich life finally reached its end, she passed away peacefully in her sleep to join her dear mentor Ignitus in the stars. The next night, Dahlia lit a lone candle in her window to honour the extraordinary soul who had kindled so much light within the world.

Though Farrah was gone, her sanctuary lived on as a testament to her life's work and selflessness. Countless lives had been irrevocably transformed by her compassion passed on through Dahlia and generations to come. Farrah's inner flame would burn eternally as a beacon in the darkness she had banished.

Farrah's sanctuary and wisdom left an indelible impact that rippled across the land. Weary souls she had cradled back to hope grew strong enough to light the way for others in turn. Soon many villages had their own beacons guiding people through darkness.

Sprites, fairies, elves and woodland beings from all corners told stories of a healer whose profound empathy and creativity reignited even the most battered spirits. Parents would hush crying children by saying "Hush now, the kind candle lady whose love outshines even the sun will always help you."

But Farrah measured her life not through accolades, only through the light rekindled within once-hollow souls who had arrived at her sanctuary feeling alone and hopeless. Watching them emerge renewed and purposeful was the only recognition she needed.

To those whose inner wells had run dry, Farrah was a garden after endless drought. For those lost and wandering the forest, she was the moon lighting the way until dawn. There was no darkness so deep that her care could not brighten lost souls back to wholeness.

As seasons turned, Farrah's comforting voice reached more each year through her writings, though her humble sanctuary remained a pilgrimage site. "When your nights feel endless, know I have wept too," she wrote, "and yet morning always comes again."

We all pass through personal winters. But Farrah showed that even when we lose sight of our inner light, it continues burning, waiting to be nurtured back to bold brilliance. She lit the way forward for all those who felt hope had perished forever, giving the greatest gift - faith that dawn will come again.

And so Farrah's singular legacy endured down generations -

the quiet miracle of one candle whose compassion and wisdom transformed despair into dawn, kindling endless lights to push back the darkness wherever it lingered. Just as she wished upon glowing fireflies long ago, her small flame blazed on eternally as a beacon guiding all souls home.

Note from the Author:

Dear Reader,

If Farrah's journey resonated with you, you are not alone. Depression touches countless lives, often in profound and painful ways. These conditions thrive in secrecy and silence. By shedding light, we empower ourselves and each other.

In telling Farrah's story, I sought to capture an emotionally honest account of struggling with mental health - the isolation, despair, exhaustion and miscommunications with loved ones. Her fantastical fairy tale setting allowed me to explore timeless truths through metaphor.

Farrah's kingdom represents our inner landscape. The dark forest she gets lost in depicts depression's chilling fog. Ignitus the phoenix embodies hope, wisdom and compassion - all within us if we search deep enough. Farrah's wings symbolize the parts of ourselves we must nurture to rise up again.

Mental health challenges manifest uniquely in each individual, but common patterns exist. Here I will share a general overview of depression and anxiety's causes, symptoms and treatments. Please know that evidence-based resources and professional support are abundantly available.

Causes

- Genetics - Depression and anxiety disorders often run in families, suggesting the inheritability of certain predispositions.
- Brain chemistry - Imbalances in neurotransmitters like serotonin may contribute to mood disorders. Environment and experiences also shape neurochemistry.
- Trauma and stress - High levels of trauma, loss, chronic stress or conflict can trigger or worsen depression and anxiety.
- Medical conditions - Conditions like thyroid disease, chronic pain, or insomnia may increase the risk for mental health issues.

Symptoms of Depression:

- Sadness, emptiness, hopelessness
- Loss of interest in usually pleasurable activities
- Fatigue, low energy, feeling "slowed down"
- Changes in appetite and sleep
- Difficulty concentrating, Increased Irritability
- Physical aches and pains, digestive issues
- Thoughts of death or suicide
- Anxiety, panic attacks, constant worrying

What Can Help:

- Finding the right therapy approach, like cognitive behavioural therapy (CBT) helps change negative thought patterns. Don't get discouraged if it takes time to find the best fit.
- Healthy lifestyle habits - Eating nutritious food, getting exercise, quality sleep, spending time outdoors and limiting social media use can improve mood over time.
- Developing mindfulness through meditation, yoga and deep breathing. Calming your mind and body has real benefits.
- Reaching out for support from friends, family, teachers, coaches, youth groups and crisis hotlines. You are never alone.
- Channelling emotions into creative outlets like art, music, writing and dance. Finding positive forms of self-expression can be incredibly helpful.
- Considering alternative approaches like equine therapy, acupuncture, craniosacral therapy, silent counselling and thought therapy. These may complement other treatments.
- Knowing that lots of support and resources exist. Never lose hope. With time and care, inner light can emerge from the darkness.

Most important is extending the same compassion to yourself that you would a friend facing similar struggles. Getting outside for fresh air, taking a bath, watching a favourite movie, or just resting matters just as much as being productive. Honour what feels right emotionally in each moment. Believe you have the courage and strength to take things moment by moment, honouring where you're at.

If you relate to Farrah's journey, know that with time, support and inner work, the fog can gradually lift to reveal a blue sky ahead. You have inner strength, courage and light even if it's hard to feel right now. Wherever you may be, you are not alone. Your light matters profoundly.

With hope and care,

Gail